a **MISFITZ** mystery

THree DiaMoNds aNd a DonkEy

Josh Lacey was born in London. He is the eldest of seven children. He now lives in London with his wife and their daughter.

He worked as a journalist, a screenwriter and a teacher before publishing his first novel for children, *A Dog Called Grk*.

You can find out more about him and his books at:
www.joshlacey.com

Also by Josh Lacey

Misfitz Mysteries
The One That Got Away
Two Tigers on a String

Bearkeeper

Writing as Joshua Doder
The Grk Series
A Dog Called Grk
Grk and the Pelotti Gang
Grk and the Hot Dog Trail
Grk: Operation Tortoise
Grk Smells a Rat

Praise for Josh Lacey's novels:

THE ONE THAT GOT AWAY

"Those who love Enid Blyton will fall on this with glee, especially because it's much better written."
Amanda Craig, *The Times*

"Plenty of humour and pace . . . an absolute must read."
Julia Eccleshare, *Lovereading4kids.co.uk*

BEARKEEPER

"A highly enjoyable read"
Guardian

"*Bearkeeper* informs as it entertains and intrigues as it enlightens"
FT

"Boys of 9+ will love Josh Lacey's *Bearkeeper*. . . The humour and wisdom of his tale will win [the author] new fans"
The Times

"There is enough here to keep readers glued to the page and to provide them with an enthralling introduction to 17th-century England"
Books for Keeps

"A most engaging and powerfully dramatic adventure . . . you cannot go wrong with *Bearkeeper*. We recommend it firmly"
Bookbag

a MISFITZ mystery

THree DiaMoNds aNd a DonkEy

JOSH LACEY

MARION LLOYD BOOKS

First published in the UK in 2010 by Marion Lloyd Books
An imprint of Scholastic Children's Books
Euston House, 24 Eversholt Street
London, NW1 1DB, UK
A division of Scholastic Ltd.
Registered office: Westfield Road, Southam, Warwickshire, CV47 0RA
SCHOLASTIC and associated logos are trademarks and/or registered
trademarks of Scholastic Inc.

ISBN 9781407109794

A CIP catalogue record for this book is
available from the British Library

Printed and bound in Great Britain by
CPI Bookmarque, Croydon
Papers used by Scholastic Children's Books are made from wood grown
in sustainable forests.

1 3 5 7 9 10 8 6 4 2

This is a work of fiction. Names, characters, places, incidents and
dialogues are products of the author's imagination or are used fictitiously.
Any resemblance to actual people, living or dead, events or locales is
entirely coincidental.

www.scholastic.co.uk/zone

To Esther

BEN'S FAMILY

Celia ← New Girlfriend

Martha
American Poet
Never Actually Married

Dad
Robot this
Divorced Ages Ago

Mum
Jennifer Fitzroy
Married
Also Divorced Ages Ago

Jeremy Fitzroy
my stepfather

Nina
lives in Bristol

Dutch
my brother
no one knows where he is

Harmony
my sister

ME

Kit Kat
the youngest

Frank
my step brother

1

Jennifer delivered them to the airport. She would have taken them right to the door of the plane, but only passengers with boarding passes were allowed to go through security. She hugged each of them in turn, first Kitkat, then Harmony, Ben and Frank. Then she grabbed her youngest daughter once more and held her as if she never wanted to let go.

Harmony glanced at her watch. "Mum, we'll miss the plane."

Jennifer reluctantly released Kitkat. "You're going to be safe, aren't you?"

"Of course we are," said Harmony. "We're perfectly capable of looking after ourselves."

"It's not *you* that I'm worried about," said Jennifer. "It's your father. He'll probably lose you. Or forget you. Or do something appalling which gets you all thrown in prison."

"That sounds cool," said Ben. "I've never been in prison."

"Well, your father has. Several times. And, I can tell you, it is not cool at all."

"Sounds cool to me."

"Wait till you're on the phone to the embassy, trying to get him released. Then it will seem like the worst day of your entire life. And, I can tell you, I had some very bad days when I was married to your father."

"Mum," said Harmony, glancing at her watch again.

"Yes, yes, I know. You'd better go. Goodbye, darlings. Have a wonderful holiday. Don't drink the water. Remember to wash your hands before meals. And, whatever you do, don't let your father get you in trouble."

There was another round of kissing and hugging and goodbyes; then the four children walked through the doorway marked DEPARTURES.

Harmony showed their passports and boarding cards to the guard, who nodded them past. They waved a final farewell to their mother and joined the queue for the X-ray machines.

2

Five hours later and three thousand kilometres further south, they emerged through a doorway marked ARRIVALS.

Harmony led the way. As soon as the plane had landed, she had wrapped her scarf around her head, covering her hair and shielding her face. She knew that women dressed like this in Morocco and she didn't want to offend the locals by behaving differently.

Just behind her came Ben, wheeling a trolley laden with all their luggage.

Kitkat was riding another trolley, pushed by Frank.

A large crowd had assembled to meet the plane from London. Families hurried forward to greet long-lost sons and daughters. Hotel representatives were holding signs to greet their guests. Tour guides were touting for custom and taxi drivers were searching for tourists who needed a ride to the centre of the city.

Harmony stood on tiptoes and peered over the tops of people's heads, searching for her dad.

Ben said, "Can you see him?"

"Not yet," said Harmony. "But he must be here somewhere."

Frank had never met Robert Amis and Kitkat hadn't seen him for years, but they looked for him too, staring at every middle-aged man in the crowd, wondering which of them might be Ben and Harmony's father. Was he that tubby chap with a flowery shirt unbuttoned to his navel? Or that handsome man in a baggy linen suit? Or that bald bloke with dark glasses hiding his eyes?

Robert Amis was American. About twenty years ago, he came to London and ran a very successful theatre company.

He met Jennifer. They got married and had two children, Harmony and Ben. Then things went wrong. They divorced and Robert went back to America.

Now he lived in Los Angeles, where he worked as a film producer. The money was better, he said, and the weather too. His films were never very successful, but he still had a Porsche and a big house with a pool.

Harmony and Ben went to stay with him almost every year. He took them to Disneyland and Venice Beach and fancy restaurants where they saw famous movie stars eating at the other tables.

This year, he had invited them to spend half-term with him and his girlfriend in Morocco. Ben and Harmony asked if Frank and Kitkat could come too and Robert said yes.

The six of them were going to stay in a smart hotel in Marrakech for a couple of nights, then drive to the Atlas Mountains and explore the wilderness. Robert had already hired a guide, some tents and several donkeys to carry all their stuff.

But where was he?

Harmony and Ben had searched every face in the airport, but there was no sign of their father.

"Why don't you call him?" suggested Frank.

"I can't afford it," said Ben. "I don't have enough credit on my phone."

"Use mine. It's free." Frank handed over his own phone.

"Why is it free?"

"I've piggybacked a local network and made it think I'm a superuser."

Ben didn't have a clue what Frank meant, but he

was sure it couldn't be legal. "Are you allowed to do that?"

"Do you want to use it or not?"

Ben took the phone and tapped in his dad's number. The call went straight to answerphone. He left a message, asking where he was and saying that they were waiting at the airport.

Frank said, "Is he often late?"

"Usually," said Harmony.

"Always," said Ben. "He used to drive Mum mad. Do you remember the time we had to wait a whole day for him?"

"I'm never going to forget that," said Harmony.

"He said he'd pick us up after breakfast," explained Ben. "But he didn't get there till supper time. Mum was so cross, she said she'd cut off his—"

"There!" Kitkat suddenly shouted.

The others turned to see what she was pointing at.

On the other side of the crowd, an unusually tall Moroccan man was holding a long piece of brown cardboard scrawled with seven big black letters:

MISFITZ

Harmony said, "Do you think that's for us?"

"How many Misfitz are there in the world?" said Kitkat. Without waiting for an answer, she threw her arms in the air and yelled at the top of her voice: "HEY! OVER HERE! WE'RE THE MISFITZ!"

Half the people in the airport turned to see who was making so much noise, but Kitkat wasn't embarrassed. She just kept shouting and waving till the man noticed her.

There may have been other Misfitz in the world, but Ben, Frank, Harmony and Kitkat were certainly the only Misfitz in Marrakech Airport. The tall Moroccan man must have known that, because he waved back and started pushing through the crowd.

You probably know already why the four of them were called the Misfitz. If you don't, have a look at the family tree at the front of this book.

You'll see that Ben, Harmony, Frank and Kitkat were brothers and sisters, but they shared two mothers (Jennifer and Nina) and two fathers (Jeremy and Robert).

Ben and Harmony were the children of Robert Amis. Jeremy Fitzroy was the father of Frank and Kitkat. In other words, they were half Amis and half Fitzroy.

When you mixed them together, you got the Misfitz.

That was what Kitkat said, anyway, and the others decided not to disagree with her. If you want to know how it all happened, you should read *The One That Got Away* and find out the whole story.

The tall Moroccan man bowed his head and leaned forward, bringing himself closer to their level. He spoke English with a strong French accent. "Bonjour. Good afternoon. Welcome to Marrakech." He smiled at Kitkat. "You are Mademoiselle 'Armony?"

"No, I'm Kitkat. She's Harmony."

The man turned his attention to Harmony. "Bonjour, Mademoiselle 'Armony. My name is Mohammed. I am sent by your father."

"He was meant to be here," said Harmony. "What's happened to him?"

"He is in the Riad Gazelle."

"What's the Riad Gazelle?"

"It is where he stays. And where you will stay also. Please, you must come with me now."

Harmony looked at Mohammed, wondering whether to trust him. Had he really been sent by their father? Or was he just a mysterious stranger who had decided to kidnap four foreign children and their luggage? She could have asked the others what they thought, but Harmony preferred to make these decisions alone. She was the oldest, after all, and much more sensible than her silly baby sister or her gormless younger brothers. She inspected Mohammed's face, searching for any sign of criminal intentions. Finally she nodded. "Come on, then. Let's go to the Riad Gazelle."

Mohammed offered to carry Harmony's suitcase, but she wouldn't let him. "I'm perfectly capable of carrying it myself, thank you."

"You can carry mine if you want," said Kitkat. "But I have to warn you, it's really heavy."

"No problem," said Mohammed, scooping up her pink suitcase as if it was weightless. "This way, please. You must follow me."

3

A battered old taxi was parked on a double yellow line directly outside the airport. The little car hardly looked big enough to fit Mohammed and his long legs, let alone four more kids and all their luggage, but he somehow managed to squeeze everyone inside. Ben, Frank and Harmony sat in a row on the back seat. Kitkat balanced on their laps, surrounded by bags. Mohammed piled the rest of the luggage in the boot, then slammed the doors and fitted himself into the front seat alongside the driver. He called back to them, "All is comfortable?"

"We're perfect, thank you," replied Harmony.

"Very good."

Mohammed muttered to the driver in Arabic. The taxi lurched forward.

The journey into town took fifteen minutes. They drove first through the modern outer suburbs, then passed under a crumbling archway and arrived in a network of narrow streets. This was the medina, the old city, the heart of Marrakech.

As soon as the Misfitz stepped out of the car, their nostrils were assaulted by cinnamon and honey and dust and drains and other, stranger scents that they couldn't identify. They could hear a neighing horse and a screaming baby and women arguing in high-pitched voices. Two boys swept past on mopeds, trailing clouds of acrid black smoke.

Ben, Harmony and Kitkat stared at their surroundings, absorbing the city's strangeness. They had never been anywhere which looked so different to their own home.

Frank wasn't so excited. He'd seen it all before. He had never been to Marrakech, but he'd travelled to India with his mother and Morocco looked just the same.

"We must walk from here," said Mohammed. He led them through a series of alleyways too thin to fit a car, turning left and right so often that none of them had any idea where they might be. Their suitcases dragged and bounced on the rough ground. They wanted to inspect everything – a mosque, an archway covered in intricate carvings, a shop selling hundreds of leather slippers – but they were careful to keep up with their guide. If they lost sight of him, they would never find their way out of this labyrinth.

Mohammed stopped at a tall wooden door studded with rusty iron rivets. He rapped twice with his knuckles.

The door was opened by a woman wearing a curious mixture of Western and Moroccan clothes: pointed gold shoes, designer jeans, a silk blouse and a mauve scarf wrapped around her head, covering her hair. She smiled at the Misfitz as if they were old friends. "Ah, *les enfants sont arrivés*! Hello, good afternoon, welcome to the Riad Gazelle. My name is Samira. I am the manager here. Please to come inside. Your papa, he is waiting."

On the other side of the doorway, they found themselves in a small, quiet courtyard, surrounded by greenery. Ochre pots held orange and lemon trees laden with fruit. Two canaries chirruped in a cage. Water cascaded from a stone fountain and frothed in a square pool filled with tiny darting goldfish.

And here was Robert, hurrying down the stairs and rushing across the courtyard, his arms outstretched, his long white dressing grown flapping around his bare legs, his face breaking open in a big grin and his deep voice booming out:

"Ben! Harmony! At last!"

Robert Amis had a long thin nose, a deep tan and curly black hair. He was an energetic, excitable man who always looked as if he'd drunk too many cups of coffee.

"I'm so sorry we didn't come to the airport, but we needed that extra hour asleep. Blame the jet lag. Blame the beds. They're too comfortable. You'll see for yourself in a minute. You're going to love this place, it's a peach."

Robert wrapped Ben and Harmony in his strong arms.

"It's so great to see you! I've missed you. Have you missed me?"

Without waiting for an answer, he released them and turned to the other two children.

"You must be Frank, hello, I'm Robert, their dad. And you're Katherine, aren't you? We've met before, years ago, you probably don't remember, you were very small. You look so much older. I do too, right? Don't answer that. Ah, this is great, I'm so pleased to see you. Welcome to Marrakech. Let's get you settled. You're going to love your rooms.

They're very special. Samira, can someone help them with their bags?"

"Yes, of course." Samira clapped her hands and called out, "Mohammed!"

"Hey! Look who's here! You've arrived!" A high-pitched Californian voice trilled across the courtyard, followed a moment later by its owner, a slim, blonde woman with high cheekbones, a neat nose and bright blue eyes. Just like Robert, she was wearing a long white dressing gown and not much else. She was twenty-five, but looked younger, and was as beautiful as a movie star. That was no surprise, because she was a movie star. Not a famous one. But she'd played small parts in several Hollywood movies, including the one where she'd met Robert. "Hello, Harmony. Remember me?"

"Of course I do," said Harmony with a tight smile. "Hello, Celia. How are you?"

"Oh, I'm fabulous." Celia pecked Harmony on both cheeks. "And look! Here's Benjy! You've grown, haven't you? What a big boy you are!" Celia wrapped her arms around Ben and gave him a tight squeeze.

Don't call me Benjy, he wanted to say. Only Mum calls me that. But he kept quiet and allowed himself to be hugged.

Last year, when Ben and Harmony went to stay with their father, they had spent an uncomfortable weekend with Celia, staying in a swanky hotel in Palm Springs. She lay on a lounger in her skimpy scarlet bikini, drinking cocktails and talking loudly about her new agent, her new diet and her new fitness regime.

Harmony couldn't understand why her father should have attached himself to someone so silly. She had consoled herself with the knowledge that Robert never stuck with the same woman for more than a few months, but Celia had already lasted longer than his previous girlfriends. With any luck, a week with four children would finally convince Robert to dump her.

4

If you go to Marrakech, you can stay in a big, modern hotel in the New City. Or you can venture into the crooked, confusing streets of the Old City and stay in a riad.

If you choose to stay in the New City, your big, modern hotel will be pretty much the same as any other big, modern hotel in any city on the planet. You'll have air-conditioning and room service and fifty channels on the TV in your bedroom.

But if you stay in the Old City, your riad will be unlike anywhere else in the world.

A riad is simply an old house built around a courtyard. Marrakech is full of them and hundreds have been converted into small hotels. Each one is different. Some boast luxuries beyond your wildest dreams. Others have rats running along the corridors and cockroaches lurking under the beds.

The Riad Gazelle is one of the smallest and smartest riads in the city. There are only four bedrooms, filled with unusual paintings, intricate mosaics and expensive antiques. On the top floor, there is a large roof terrace where an elegant breakfast is served in the mornings. When you're tired of traipsing around the city, looking at the sights, you can while away the afternoons on the terrace, lounging on cushions and staring at the view of the mountains.

Robert had booked the whole place. The boys had a room each, the girls shared another and Robert and Celia got the master suite.

Ben's room was twice as big as his bedroom at home. He had a wide, squashy bed, a wooden desk and a square window with a view of the courtyard. Thick carpets hung on the walls. At the far end of the room, hidden behind a heavy curtain embroidered with hundreds of tiny mirrors, there was a basin, a toilet and the biggest shower that he'd ever seen.

He unpacked his bag, took a shower and changed his clothes. He looked at his phone. It was ten to seven. They had arranged to meet downstairs in forty minutes. He thought about exploring the riad, but decided to do some preparation first. He lay on his bed and read the guidebook.

He learnt five facts about Morocco.

1 – Morocco is in Africa.

Ben had visited several countries in Europe and a few states in the USA, but he had never been to Africa before, so he was pretty excited about that.

2 – Most Moroccans speak at least three languages – Arabic, Berber and French – and many of them speak English too.

Ben could speak English, of course, and a few words of French, but no Arabic at all. He'd never even heard of Berber.

At the back of the guide, there was a section called LANGUAGE. Ben learnt how to say "Yes, please" and "No, thank you" in French and Arabic.

Oui, s'il vous plait.

Eeyeh, minfadlik.

Non, merci.

Waha, barakalayfik.

He knew the numbers in French already.

Un, deux, trois, quatre, cinq, six, sept, huit, neuf, dix.

And now he learnt them in Arabic too.

Wahed, jooq, tlata, arba, khamsa, setta, seba, tmenia, tse'ud, ashara.

He tried to memorize a few other phrases too. *What is your name? Where is the toilet? My name is Ben.* But he forgot them as soon as he'd read them.

3 – Marrakech was once the capital of a kingdom ruled by ferocious warriors, but it was now just a small, peaceful city which made much of its income from foreign tourists.

Like me, thought Ben.

Actually, that wasn't quite true. He wouldn't be spending any money at all. His dad was paying for everything.

4 – Wherever you go, you will be accosted by people offering to guide you around the city. Don't say yes. They'll usually take you to a carpet factory or a shop selling antiques and try to persuade you to buy some overpriced junk. If someone offers to guide you through the city, just politely say no and ask them to leave you alone.

That was no problem. Ben had just learnt the words for "no, thank you" in both French and Arabic. If he met any guides, he'd tell them that he preferred to find his own way around.

5 – There is a big square at the centre of Marrakech. It's called the Jemma al Fna and is one of the most amazing places on Earth, filled with dancers, musicians, storytellers and snake charmers.

Ben didn't have much experience of guidebooks, but he'd learnt not to trust them. They always made things sound more interesting than they actually were. They'd say somewhere was unbelievably beautiful or amazingly exciting, but when you got there, you'd just find yourself in a boring old museum or a big dark church.

Even so, he wanted to see the Jemma al Fna. He liked the sound of the snake charmers.

Robert had asked them to assemble in the courtyard at half past seven. He had already booked a table in a smart restaurant about five minutes' walk from the riad.

Ben was precisely on time. When he came downstairs, only Frank was there, sitting in a chair by the fountain, working on his computer.

"Hiya," said Ben. "How's your room?"

"Fine," grunted Frank without lifting his eyes from the screen.

"Mine's huge. It's got to be twice as big as my room at home. And the bed is so comfortable! I feel like I could sleep for a hundred years. Do you know what I mean?"

"No."

Frank was a boy of few words.

While Ben wandered round the courtyard, inspecting the lemon trees and peering at the fish in the fountain, Frank continued working on his computer as if he was alone.

Ben knew that Frank didn't really want to be here. He'd have preferred to stay at home. But his mum had gone to Venice with her new boyfriend, an artist called Dominic, and Frank wasn't allowed to stay in their flat on his own.

Kitkat and Harmony came downstairs next. Robert arrived at quarter to eight, followed ten minutes later by Celia, apologizing to everyone for her lateness. "I couldn't decide which skirt to wear. What do you think? Was this the right choice?" She did a twirl, showing off her outfit, an elegant white blouse and a willowy silk skirt embroidered with tiny flowers.

"I love it!" Kitkat clapped her hands. "That's beautiful!"

"Very nice," said Harmony in a crisp tone.

The boys didn't have any opinion.

Mohammed had been waiting patiently in the kitchen. He was going to lead them to the restaurant, which was hidden away in the backstreets, impossible to find unless you knew the way.

They were just about to leave when Robert realized that Frank was carrying his computer. "What do you need that for?"

"It's my computer," said Frank, as if that explained everything.

"We're going out to dinner. Why do you need a computer?"

"I'd like to have it with me. If you don't mind."

"I do mind," said Robert. "Dinner is for conversation, not computers. We're human beings, not machines. Will you take it back to your room, please?"

"I'd rather bring it," said Frank.

"I'd rather you didn't. You can stay here with your computer or you can leave it here and come with us. The choice is yours."

"Then I'll stay here."

Frank didn't want to be pushed around by a man who wasn't his father or even his stepfather, just the father of his stepbrother and his stepsister. As for Robert – well, he saw no reason to indulge the whims of a spoilt young brat. Neither of them was going to back down and so there was only one way that their disagreement could end: Frank stayed in the riad with his computer. Samira promised to find him some supper. The others followed

Mohammed out of the heavy wooden door and into the streets.

They walked in single file, plunging through a bewildering sequence of shabby roads and unlit passageways. They passed a blind beggar rattling coins in a little brass bowl and a pair of dogs fighting in the dust and an old man sitting on a step, plucking notes from a long-necked guitar with only four strings. Finally they arrived at a tall, gold door. Two men in black uniforms stood guard with stern expressions and folded arms.

"*Voilà*," said Mohammed. "La Porte d'Or."

"What does that mean?" asked Kitkat.

"What do you think?" said Harmony.

"If I knew, I wouldn't be asking."

"It means *the golden door*. Because the door is—"

"I get it," said Kitkat. "You don't have to explain everything."

La Porte d'Or is the best restaurant in Marrakech. There is nowhere better if you want to taste the finest Moroccan delicacies. That was what Robert had been told, anyway, so he had rung ahead from Los Angeles and booked a table.

Mohammed offered to stay outside the restaurant and guide them back to the Riad Gazelle when they finished their meal, but Robert told him not to bother.

"I have a photographic memory," Robert explained. "I can remember where I've been and what I've seen. When I've driven a route once – or walked it – I can always find my way back along the same route."

"How do you know how to do that?" asked Ben.

"I don't know." Robert shrugged his shoulders modestly. "It's just a special skill that I've been blessed with."

One of the guards checked Robert's reservation in a large leather-bound book. Then the other guard pulled the door open and ushered everyone into La Porte d'Or.

5

A hundred candles flickered in niches along the walls. At the end of a long corridor, they entered a dimly lit dining room hung with velvet drapes, and a waiter bowed to them. "*Bon soir, Monsieur Amis. Votre table est prêt. Suivez-moi, s'il vous plaît.*"

The five of them sat on the floor and ate from a low wooden table. Robert would have preferred a chair, but the others were comfortable sprawling on big cushions.

They were served course after course of Moroccan food, starting with bowls of little green olives and a plate of pickled vegetables. Next came pigeon pastilla. (A pastilla, they were told by the waiter, is a kind of pie.) Then they were given two types of tagine, the first made with chicken and lemons, the next with lamb and prunes. (A tagine, said the waiter, is a Moroccan stew, served in a special earthenware pot with a cone-shaped lid.)

Musicians sat in one corner of the restaurant, tapping small drums and plucking at a harp, and a belly dancer wove between the tables, waggling her hips.

Midway through the meal, Robert cleared his throat. "Listen up, kids. I have an important announcement to make." His eyes roamed around the table, lingering for a moment on Ben and Harmony. Then he took his girlfriend's hand in both of his. "Last night, I asked a question of this wonderful woman. There are many questions that a man can ask a woman, but this is probably the most important of them all. To my delight, she said yes. Kids, I'd like you to welcome a new member to the family. Celia and I are getting married."

Harmony choked on a chickpea. Ben stared open-mouthed at his father. Even Kitkat was lost for words. And then they remembered their manners. They congratulated the bride-to-be, hurrying around the table to embrace her.

Ben congratulated his father too. "Good luck, Dad."

"Third time lucky," added Harmony.

"Second, actually," said Robert. "I've only married once before."

"You've had lots of girlfriends."

"A few. But I've never wanted to marry any of them."

"You wanted to marry Mum," said Ben.

"We all make mistakes." Robert laughed, then noticed that neither of his children were laughing with him. "Sorry, kids. That was a bad joke. Forget I said it."

"Don't worry," said Ben. "Mum says much worse things about you."

The smile disappeared from Robert's face. "Like what?"

"I couldn't possibly tell you," said Ben.

There was an awkward silence. No one knew what to say. Robert watched his children nervously and Celia started eating quickly as if she couldn't wait for the meal to be over.

Kitkat was the first to speak. "Where are you going to get married?"

"That's an excellent question," said Celia, putting down her fork and daintily wiping her lips with her napkin. "I was born in South Dakota and my dad's still there, but I only go back to see him at Christmas and Thanksgiving. And your dad's a New Yorker, of course. But we both live in California and so do most of our friends, so that seems the most logical place to have a party."

"Will you invite any movie stars?" asked Kitkat.

"One or two," said Robert.

"Can I come?"

"I'll be offended if you don't."

"How about Frank? Is he invited?"

"Of course he is," said Robert. "As long as he doesn't bring his computer."

"Then he won't want to come," said Ben.

Robert rolled his eyes. "Fine, his computer can have an invitation too. It can even have a seat at the dinner. I want all four of you to be there."

There was another awkward silence. Harmony pushed food around her plate and Ben stared at the ceiling. They were wondering whether having a stepmother would make any difference to their lives. Probably not. They only saw their father for a week or two each year. But they couldn't understand why, of all the women in the world, Robert should have picked Celia for his second wife.

Once again, Kitkat broke the silence. "Do you have a ring?"

"Of course," said Celia.

"Can I see?"

Celia stretched her arm across the table, showing off the thick silver band on her left hand. It was studded with three enormous diamonds.

Kitkat begged to be allowed to try it on.

"It won't fit you," said Celia. "My fingers are much larger than yours and the ring's too big even for me. I need to have it altered when we get back home." But when she saw the disappointment on Kitkat's face, she slid the ring off her finger and passed it across the table.

Kitkat squeaked with excitement, slipping the ring on to each of her fingers and both her thumbs too, trying it for size. She offered her outstretched hand to the others for their approval. "What do you think? Does it suit me?"

"It's very nice," said Harmony, managing to sound as if she meant the exact opposite.

Kitkat turned to Celia. "Where did you get it? Tiffany's?"

"A very special little store in Paris," said Celia. "You can't fly direct from Los Angeles to Marrakech, so we had to change planes in France. Your father suggested we stay for a night. I didn't realize he was going to take me to a jewellery store."

When Kitkat had gasped and cooed enough, Celia offered the ring to the others. Harmony took a quick look, then passed the ring to Ben. He placed it in the palm of his hand and pored over the diamonds, watching the candlelight shimmer and sparkle on the three finely cut gems.

Ben had never seen such enormous diamonds. He was curious to know how much the ring was worth, but he felt embarrassed asking his dad about money.

Kitkat didn't have any such inhibitions. "Was it expensive?"

"Very," said Robert.

"How much?"

Celia giggled and Robert smiled. "I'm not going to tell you the price," he said. "But I will tell you this. Apart from my house, I have never bought anything more expensive in my entire life."

6

After supper, they walked out of the restaurant and headed for the riad. Robert led the way. He took them through a series of narrow alleyways, striding quickly and confidently as if he walked the same route every day.

They came to a crossroads.

Every direction looked the same, but Robert told them not to worry. "I have a photographic memory," he reminded them. "Our route has been seared on my neurons. It's down here. We'll be home in a second. Come on, kids. Follow me!"

There were no street lights in the narrow alleys. Low clouds wisped across the sky, parting occasionally to give glimpses of the stars.

A black cat followed them for a few paces, then slipped into the shadows and faded away. The chatter of televisions boomed from upstairs windows. Several men were standing in a doorway, talking in low voices. In the darkness, the tips of their cigarettes gleamed like eyes.

They turned another corner and a salesman blocked their way, trying to entice them into his shop. He was an old man with a grey beard and a funny little red hat tucked on the back of his head. "You want carpet? Good carpet? Cheap price!" He grabbed Robert's sleeve. "Come! Look! No buying, just looking."

"Maybe tomorrow," said Robert, tugging himself free.

"Good carpet! Cheap price! Best price!" The old man's voice pursued them as they continued down the dark alleyway.

Robert turned a corner, then another, and paused at the next crossroads. He seemed less confident now. He looked both ways as if he was searching for something, then pointed to the right. "I think it's down here."

"You *think*?" said Harmony. "Dad, are you lost?"

"You're joking, right? I've already told you, I don't get lost."

"So you know where you're going?"

"Of course I do. Didn't you hear what I just said? It's down here. Come on, kids, quick march. Not long now. We're almost home."

He led them down the alleyway. They passed a trio of German tourists taking photos of a wrought-iron lantern hanging outside a shuttered shop. Round the next corner, they met a group of teenage girls with a tiny black puppy. Celia stopped to pat his head and tickle his ears. "He's such a sweetie! What's his name?"

None of the girls could speak English, but they must have understood what Celia meant, because one of them blurted out, "Leila! Leila!" The others giggled and whispered, hiding their faces behind their shawls.

"That's a cute puppy," said Robert. "But let's keep moving. We don't want to spend all night out here."

They walked for a long time through indistinguishable alleyways, past shops selling slippers and shops selling lanterns and shops selling crockery and shops selling just about anything else that you could possibly want, and then they came to a carpet shop owned by an old man with a grey beard and a funny little red hat tucked on the back of his head. He smiled and beckoned them inside. "You want good carpet? Come, look. I have best carpet for you. Please, you are my guest. Just looking, no buying."

Robert hurried past as if he hadn't even noticed

the carpet shop and led his family further down the street.

"I recognize him," said Kitkat, looking back at the old man.

"That's because we've been here before," said Harmony. "We're walking round in circles."

Robert chuckled. "You're just confused. All these shops look the same."

"Oh, come off it, Dad. We're not idiots. You don't have a clue where we are, do you?"

Robert looked at his daughter, considering whether to bluff, then realized that there was no point. "I know what's happened. We must have taken the wrong turning at the crossroads. Last time we were there, I felt something in my gut. An unease, you know what I mean? It's a lesson to me. I should always take more notice of my intuitions. This time, we'll go left rather than right. We'll be home in two seconds."

"We're lost," said Harmony. "Why can't you admit it?"

"I'm not lost," said Robert. "I just don't know where we are right now."

"What's the difference?"

Robert sighed. "Fine. I'm lost. There, I've said it. Are you happy now?"

"Of course not," said Harmony. "I don't *want* to be lost. I'd much rather be back in the hotel."

"We will be soon. We just have to walk a bit further."

"That's what you said about an hour ago. Since then we've been walking round and round in circles."

"I'm tired," whined Kitkat. "My feet hurt."

"Mine too," said Celia. "These shoes are agony. I wouldn't have worn heels if I'd known we were going to be hiking."

"Let's turn round," suggested Ben. "We could go back to that carpet shop and ask the old guy for directions."

"No, no," said Robert. "You should never turn back. Onwards, ever onwards. That's always been my motto. Let's keep going, kids. We'll be home in no time, I guarantee it."

"You want guide?" said a voice.

A small, skinny boy was standing in the middle of the street, smiling at them. He seemed to have appeared from nowhere, but he might have been there for ages, watching their argument and waiting for the perfect moment to intervene.

Robert said, "Who are you?"

"I am guide," said the boy. He had a cheeky,

confident face and an irresistible toothy smile. He was wearing ragged trousers, an old cotton shirt, a dirty grey hoodie and battered leather sandals which couldn't have given much protection to his bare feet. "You want guide?"

"No, thank you," said Robert. "We don't need a guide."

"We definitely need a guide," said Harmony. "We want to get back to our hotel. It's called the Riad Gazelle. Do you know it?"

The boy nodded. "Yes, yes, no problem. The Riad Gazelle is this way." He took two paces down the alley. "You follow me, please."

"I already told you," said Robert. "We don't need a guide."

Ben remembered the advice in his guidebook. This scruffy boy must be one of those guides who pretends to show you round the city, but actually takes you to his cousin's carpet shop and persuades you to buy an overpriced rug. He considered warning his dad, but decided not to bother. Visiting a carpet shop would be a thousand times more fun than following his father round and round and round and round in circles for half the night.

Harmony had reached the same conclusion. "He

knows where he's going, Dad. He lives here. We might as well follow him."

Robert couldn't believe it. "Given the choice between your own father and a complete stranger, you'd rather follow a stranger?"

"Sorry, Dad. It's nothing personal. But I don't want to spend the whole night out here."

"Don't speak too soon." Robert turned to the boy. "What's your name?"

"Tariq."

"Tell me something, Tariq. How much are you planning to charge us for this little bit of guidance?"

"No money," said Tariq. "Just friendship."

"I like your attitude," said Robert. "You're a good salesman. Go on, then. Get us back to the riad. If you're quick, I might even give you a tip."

7

Tariq walked fast, never hesitating and not saying a word, just turning his head every few paces to check that they were behind him.

They hadn't been walking for more than three or four minutes when he delivered them to a wooden door studded with rusty iron bolts.

"Here is where you are," said Tariq. "La Riad Gazelle."

Kitkat whooped. Ben clapped. Harmony said, "Thank you, Tariq. Thank you so much. You're a genius."

"No problem," said Tariq. "*Mon plaisir*. I am always happy to be help."

"I was wrong," said Robert. "The kids were right. And I'm big enough to admit it. Tariq, we're very grateful. Thank you for your help." He opened his wallet, selected a grubby banknote and thrust it into Tariq's hand.

The note was only a hundred dirhams, barely enough to buy a sandwich in London or Los Angeles, but it must have been much more than Tariq had expected, because he tucked the money into his shorts, then pumped Robert's hand and thanked him effusively. "*Merci bien, monsieur. Merci beaucoup.* From the bottom of my heart, my good sir, I am saying thank you."

"It's my pleasure," said Robert. "We're just delighted to be home."

Tariq turned to Celia and thanked her too. "*Merci beaucoup, madame.* Thank you so much." He clasped her hand in both of his. "Your husband is a good man, a kind man. Thank you, thank you. A thousand times I say thank you."

"Don't mention it," said Celia, giggling and glancing at Robert.

"They're not actually married," said Harmony.

"It doesn't matter," said Celia. "We will be soon."

Tariq released her hand and turned to the others. "I thank you too. I thank you all." He wished them a very good night and hurried away, melting into the shadows at the end of the alley.

"What a sweet boy," said Celia.

"I liked him too," said Kitkat. "He had a nice face."

Ben remembered what the guidebook had said. Well, it had been quite wrong. Tariq had brought them directly to their destination. And he hadn't even mentioned carpets.

Ben wasn't surprised. He'd begun to suspect that guidebooks were written by people who never even visited the countries that they were writing about. They probably just stayed at home and read other guidebooks.

Robert knocked on the heavy wooden door. They had to wait a few moments; then the door creaked open and Mohammed peered out. When he saw them, his face lit up with a delighted smile. "*Bon soir, Monsieur Amis! Bon soir, madame. Et les enfants, bon soir.* How is your dinner?"

"It was delicious, thank you," said Robert. "And we've had a fascinating stroll back home, seeing the streets of your beautiful city."

"You did not get lost?"

"Dad has a photographic memory," said Harmony. "He never gets lost."

"I am very glad to hear this." Mohammed ushered them into the riad, then closed the wooden door and locked it with two long metal bolts.

In the courtyard, Frank was sitting at a table, hunched over a chessboard. He was midway through a game with Mohammed. He gave them a quick wave, then returned his attention to the pieces.

Mohammed said, "You will take some tea with mint?"

Everyone said yes except Celia, who wanted to go straight to bed. "It might be the middle of the night here, but it's the middle of the afternoon in Los Angeles and my body really can't make sense of that. Goodnight, everyone. Sleep tight. Don't let the bedbugs bite. See you in the morning." She blew them a kiss and hurried up the stairs to the bedrooms.

They gathered around the chessboard.

Ben said, "Who's winning?"

"Five-one to me," replied Frank.

"He beat you once? He must be good."

"I played that game with my eyes shut."

Robert's competitive instincts had been aroused. "You want a game? I haven't played for a while, but I used to be pretty good."

"Sure," said Frank. "If Mohammed doesn't mind finishing this game early?"

"No problem," said Mohammed, relieved to have escaped so lightly. He disappeared into the kitchen to brew some mint tea.

The others grabbed chairs and sat beside the fountain. Tiny goldfish flickered in the dark water, swimming among a few bronze and silver coins. Frank set up the pieces.

"We've got a free day tomorrow," said Robert. "We can wander round the town. Go shopping. Visit a museum. Or just chill out here and enjoy the sunshine. This is your holiday, you can choose. What do you want to do?"

"I'd like to visit the Jemma al Fna," said Ben.

"We'll go there straight after breakfast," said Robert. "You can't come to Marrakech without seeing the Jemma al Fna. Anyone else?"

"I want to look inside a mosque," said Harmony.

"I'm sure we can arrange that. Any other suggestions?"

"I want to buy some slippers," said Kitkat. "I know which ones. I've seen a picture. They're pink and they have gold embroidery round the sides. They're absolutely gorgeous!"

"We'll search the souk for them."

"What's the souk?" asked Kitkat.

"The market. That's just what they call it here."

Frank offered two closed fists to Robert. "You can choose."

"That one."

Frank opened his fist to reveal a white pawn.

Robert said, "So I start, right?"

"Indeed," said Frank.

"Excellent. Let's get this show on the road." Robert plucked the pawn from Frank's fist and placed it on the board, then pushed it two squares forward. "What did you have for supper, Frank?"

Frank moved one of his own pawns before replying. "Soup."

Robert scratched his chin and stared at the board. His hand wavered over a pawn, then moved a knight. "What sort of soup?"

"Vegetable."

"How was it?"

"Delicious, thank you." Frank moved his own knight. "I also had some nice cheese and a piece of—"

A loud scream cut through the air.

Frank stopped in mid-sentence, his mouth open, too surprised to say another word. He'd never heard a scream like that. Not in real life. Only in horror movies. It was the type of scream that an actress makes when she sees a madman stepping out of her closet with an evil grin and a carving knife.

"Who was that?" cried Kitkat.

"It must have been Celia," said Ben.

Robert was already running for the staircase. The others sprang out of their chairs and sprinted after him. Someone's knee thwacked against the chessboard, scattering the pieces. A pawn plopped in the fountain and sank among the fish.

Mohammed rushed out of the kitchen. When he saw the others running up the stairs, he pounded across the courtyard after them.

8

Celia was standing beside the bed. Her face was white and her eyes flickered distractedly around the room, never fixing on anyone or anything for more than a moment.

"What's wrong?" cried Robert.

"My ring." Celia's voice trembled. "My beautiful ring! It's been stolen!"

"Who took it? Where are they?" Robert strode into the room, his fists raised, ready to pounce on the intruder and wrestle him to the floor.

"There's no one here," sighed Celia.

"Which way did they go?"

"It didn't happen in this room, darling. It happened in the street. I didn't notice anything at the time, but it's the only explanation. I said goodnight to you and came upstairs and started taking off my jewellery. That was when I saw it had gone. But there's only one place it could have been taken and only one person who could have stolen it." Her voice wavered. "That boy."

"Which boy?" asked Robert.

"The one who brought us back here. He must have pulled it off my finger when he shook my hand."

"He didn't look like a thief," said Kitkat.

Celia turned on her and hissed, "How do you know what a thief looks like?"

Kitkat didn't have an answer to that.

Ben had a question. "If you don't mind me asking, how can you be so sure that the ring was actually stolen?"

"Because it was on my finger." Celia raised her left hand. "And now it's not."

"Maybe you took it off," suggested Ben. "You could have put it down and forgot where you put it."

"I may be blonde, Benjy, but I'm not dumb. Apart from that one time in the restaurant when you all looked at it, the ring stayed right here on my finger. I didn't remove it. Trust me, I'd have remembered if I had."

"You might have dropped it."

"You've never worn a ring, have you?"

"No," admitted Ben.

"If you had, you'd know that rings don't just fall off your finger. Ask the girls, they'll tell you. Rings have to be pulled off. And only one person could have done it. That boy! That infuriating little boy! I can't believe we trusted him!" Celia turned to Mohammed. "You have to help us. You have to find this boy and get my ring back. Can you do that? If you can, we'll make it worth your while."

"I do not know this boy," said Mohammed. "Who is he? What is his name?"

"How am I supposed to know?"

"His name is Tariq," said Kitkat.

Ben corrected her. "He *said* his name was Tariq. His real name might be anything."

"You met him where?" asked Mohammed.

"Some street," said Robert. "We weren't exactly sure where we were or which way to go. He said he was a guide. He brought us back here. I tipped him a hundred dirhams."

"This is too much money," said Mohammed disapprovingly. "You must tell me, please, how does he look?"

"He looks like a boy," snapped Celia. "An ordinary boy."

Mohammed shrugged his shoulders. "There are many boys in Marrakech. And many of these boys are working as guides for tourists. If you can tell me how he is looking or what is he named, then I can find him. No problem. I find him like this!" He clicked his fingers. "But if you do not know nothing, then how is it possible for me to find him?"

Ben could have described what Tariq was wearing and how he had looked, but he kept quiet. He didn't believe that Tariq was a thief. It just didn't make sense. When did he have an opportunity to take the ring? How could he have wrestled it from Celia's finger? For the moment, Ben kept these questions to himself, waiting to see what happened.

Celia turned to Robert. "Can't you do something?"

"What can I do?" said Robert.

"Find that boy and get my ring back!"

"It's not so easy. Mohammed is right. How are we supposed to find him if no one knows who he is?"

"I can't believe it! This is hopeless!" Plump tears welled in Celia's eyes and trickled down her pale cheeks. "My beautiful diamond ring! Am I never going to see it again?"

Robert wrapped her in his arms and wiped the

tears from her face. "Calm down, babe. You needn't worry. We'll find it."

"But how?" wailed Celia.

"I don't know right now, but we will find it. I promise we will."

"You should go to the police as soon as possible," said Frank. "They have to start searching the city immediately. If they can find the thief in the next few hours, he might still have the ring. But if they wait till tomorrow morning, he'll have time to break it apart. He'll sell the silver to one person and the diamonds to another. And then they'll be impossible to find. Every second counts. You should go to the police right now and tell them what's happened."

Celia looked at Frank with renewed respect. "I like your style, Frankie. You're the only one of us who's actually using his brain." She turned to Robert. "He's right, isn't he?"

"I think he is," said Robert. "Mohammed, where's the nearest police station?"

"Five minutes from here," replied Mohammed. "There is one big police station in the New City, but there is another for tourists in the Jemma al Fna. I will take you there."

9

Robert marched through the wooden doors of the police station with the others hurrying after him. It was long past their bedtimes, but they had insisted on accompanying their father and he didn't have the time or the energy to argue. He strode up to the main desk and placed his hands on the counter. "I wish to report a theft."

There was a uniformed policeman sitting behind the desk. He asked a few questions in halting English, then picked up a heavy black phone and made a call. He spoke in Arabic, so none of them could understand what he was saying. He ended the call and stood up. "You will come with me, please."

The policeman led Robert and the others down a long white corridor. They came to a closed door. The policeman knocked twice and waited for an answering shout, then went inside and had a quick conversation with the occupant.

Ben read a small brass sign fixed to the door. It was inscribed in two languages, French and Arabic. Ben could only understand the French:

INSPECTEUR BENTAHIR MAHMOUD

The policeman returned and nodded to Robert. "You will come now, please. The inspector will see you."

Inside the room, a fat man was sitting behind a wide desk. His heavy limbs were squeezed into a grey suit straining at the seams. Food stains dotted his white shirt. The culprit was laid out in front of him: a bowl of soup, a plate of pickles, two tomatoes, three red peppers, four roast chicken legs, eight brown eggs and half a loaf of white bread speckled with sesame seeds. He hauled himself to his feet and leaned across the desk to shake hands with Robert. "*Bon soir*, good evening, my name is Inspector Mahmoud. I understand you have been the victim of a thief. Please to sit down. I hope I can help you."

There were only two chairs. Robert and Celia took them and the four children lined up against the back wall.

"I am taking my dinner," said the inspector,

indicating the food spread out before him. "You will join me, perhaps? Or you will prefer some coffee?"

Robert answered for all of them. "No, thank you. We'd rather just talk. Every second counts, you know. We want to find this thief before he has a chance to leave town."

"Of course, of course." The inspector smiled reassuringly. "You must not worry, we will find him immediately. First, I need to know your names. *Monsieur?*"

"My name is Robert Amis. That's A, M, I, S."

"Very good. I am pleased to meet you, Monsieur Amis." The inspector smiled at Celia. "Madame Amis, I am pleased to meet you also."

"Actually, my name is Celia Clifton. Do you need me to spell that?"

"You are not Madame Amis?"

"Not yet," said Celia. "For now, we're just very good friends."

"You are friends?" said the inspector, pointing at her and Robert.

"That's right. We're friends."

"Very good." The inspector pointed at Harmony. "So she is your wife?"

Robert laughed. "No, no. She's my daughter."

The inspector chewed the end of his pencil, not sure what to write. "Where is your wife?"

"I don't have a wife."

"You have no wife?"

"No. I have been married, but I'm not right now."

The inspector pointed at Kitkat. "She is also your daughter?"

"No, she's the daughter of my ex-wife."

"She is the daughter of your wife?"

"Not exactly," said Robert. "She's the daughter of the woman who was once my wife, but is now married to someone else."

"Where is he?"

"Her dad? He's in London. With her mother. My ex-wife."

The inspector rubbed his head. He pointed at Ben. "And him?"

"He is my son."

Then Frank. "And him also?"

"He is the son of my ex-wife's second husband."

Inspector Mahmoud had heard enough. He put down the pencil and picked up a boiled egg. "You have one wife, you have no wife, it is no matter. Please, you will tell me what happened. What have you lost? Who took it? And how? Tell me everything." He rolled the egg on the desk, cracking its shell.

"We've lost a ring," said Robert.

"We haven't *lost* anything," interrupted Celia. "It was stolen by a boy in the street."

"He said his name was Tariq," added Ben.

"That's what he *said*," explained Kitkat. "We don't know if he was telling the truth."

Harmony said, "Of course he wasn't. Why would he tell us his real name?"

"He could have done it by mistake," suggested Frank, who had been told the whole story while they walked from the riad to the police station.

Celia stepped in with her own ideas and so did Robert and soon everyone was talking at once. Each of them had their own opinion and they all wanted to be heard, so they spoke louder and louder, arguing about Tariq, the ring, what had happened and who was responsible.

The inspector concentrated on his egg. He peeled the last scraps of shell and gathered them into a neat pile. He dipped the naked tip of the egg in a little pyramid of salt, popped the whole thing in his mouth, chewed twice and gulped it down. Then he wiped his lips with a handkerchief and clapped his hands together.

"Silence!" No one took any notice, so he clapped again and shouted even louder: "Silence, *s'il vous plaît*! Silence!"

When they were finally quiet, the inspector shook his head. "I will talk to one persons. Maybe two persons. But not all the persons at the same time. This is the way to be crazy!" He pointed at the children. "They must wait outside."

Ben protested, "But we saw just as much as—"

"*Non!*" The inspector cut him off. "I will talk with your father and the friend of your father. But no children."

"That's so unfair," said Kitkat. "We have rights too. Haven't you heard of—"

"Enough!" The inspector slammed his fist on the table. Then he turned to Robert. "They go. Or you all go. Do you understand?"

"We understand," said Robert. He looked at the four children. "I'm sorry, guys, but he's the boss. We have to obey orders. Can you wait for us in the lobby?"

"Of course we can," said Harmony.

"You'll be safe there?"

"Dad, we'll be fine. We're perfectly capable of looking after ourselves."

"That's great, thank you." Robert opened his

wallet and pulled out a hundred-dirham note. He handed it to Harmony. "Buy yourself some drinks. We'll be out in a minute. I'm sure this won't take long."

10

"Excuse me?" Kitkat rapped her knuckles on the edge of the main desk at the front of the police station. "*Monsieur?* Excuse me? Hello?"

The policeman reluctantly lifted his head from his papers and peered at her. "*Oui, mademoiselle?* You need help?"

"I need a drink," said Kitkat. "Is there a drinks machine in here?"

"Excuse me? Is there what?"

"A drinks machine. For buying drinks. You know, drink." She mimed pouring a glass down her throat. "Can we buy drinks here?"

"Outside." The policeman pointed through the wooden doors that led to the Jemma al Fna.

Kitkat returned to the others, who were sitting on a rickety old bench with thin wooden slats and no cushions. "Shall we go outside and get a drink?"

"We can't leave the police station," said Harmony.

"Why not?"

"Dad told us to wait here."

"He's not my dad."

"You're in his care. He has parental responsibility for all four of us while we're in Morocco."

"Whatever," said Kitkat. "The point is, he gave us some money for a drink. He won't mind if we go outside and get it."

"He might not mind, but I would. You're tired, Kitkat. You should be in bed. And even if it wasn't the middle of the night, you're not allowed to wander round a strange town on your own."

"You can't stop me. You're not my mother." Kitkat held out her hand. "Can I have the money?"

Harmony sighed. She reached into her pocket and fished out the hundred dirhams that she'd been given by her father. "Be careful, Kitkat. You'd better not get lost."

"I'm just going to buy a drink. Of course I won't get lost." Kitkat waggled the banknote at the others. "Free drinks! Come and get your free drinks! Anyone want a free drink?"

"Yes, please." Frank stood up.

"Me too," said Ben, joining the others.

"You can't all go," complained Harmony.

"Why not?"

"Because I'm not staying here on my own."

"Then come too."

11

They emerged from the police station and stood in the corner of the Jemma al Fna, trying to work out where to buy a drink. In the darkness, it was hard to see any shops or cafés and they weren't sure where to go. They should have asked the policeman what would be open at this time of night.

A bewildering mixture of noises filled the air – pipes and drums, songs and chants, shrieks and shouts, car horns and neighing horses – mingling together into a single wild tuneless roar.

Hundreds of bare light bulbs hung from stalls and cafés, casting a yellowish glow. People flitted in and out of the shadows, their faces hidden, their bodies disappearing into the gloom.

The centre of the square was packed with men and women, boys and girls, foreigners and locals, laughing and talking, buying and selling, performing and photographing, jostling for space with all the square's other occupants: cats and dogs, snakes and monkeys, bicycles and tricycles, mopeds and motorbikes, taxis and lorries, horse-drawn carriages and rickety wooden carts pulled by dishevelled donkeys.

Standing on the edge of this chaotic scene, it was impossible to know which way to go – or even where to look.

Frank took control. "Do you like orange juice?"

Kitkat nodded eagerly. "Yes, please."

The others did too.

"Come this way," said Frank.

On one side of the square, there was a line of twenty or thirty carts, piled high with oranges in neat pyramids. Salesmen cooed and beckoned. "You want one juice? Fresh juice! Best juice! All clean juice! Hey, you! Yes, you! Come here! I will give you very good price!"

Frank ignored them all. Somehow he knew exactly where he wanted to go. He headed for a cart in the middle of the line.

The others followed him.

Frank nodded to the salesman as if they had known one another for many years. "How much?"

"Ten dirhams for one glass," said the man

behind the counter. He was wearing an immaculate white apron and a little cloth cap. "You want? Yes? How many?"

"I'll buy four glasses for twenty dirhams," said Frank.

"No, no." The salesman chuckled as if he'd never heard anything so ridiculous in his entire life. "One glass is ten dirhams, four glasses is forty dirhams."

"If you don't want our custom," said Frank, "we can go elsewhere." He half-turned and scanned the rest of the stalls as if he was deciding which one to choose.

"Wait, wait. I give you four glasses, you give me thirty dirhams."

"Twenty dirhams," said Frank. "Or nothing."

"Twenty-five?"

"Twenty."

"No problem," said the salesman. "Four glasses, twenty dirhams. The customer is always right." He arranged four gleaming glasses in a line and filled them to the brim with orange juice.

Frank handed round the glasses. He paid the salesman and gave eighty dirhams change to Harmony.

The juice was cool and delicious. They leaned

against the counter as they drank and looked around the Jemma al Fna.

The guidebook was right. Ben had never seen such an extraordinary place. He could have stood there for hours, just watching.

On one side of the square, there were about fifty stalls, manned by chefs in white overalls offering all kinds of hot and cold food – glassy-eyed fish, deep-fried chicken wings, lamb kebabs, sizzling sausages, boiled snails and big bowls filled with tottering pyramids of chopped tomato, pepper, carrot and cucumber. As diners wandered between the stalls, choosing where to eat, the chefs shouted to them, promising that their food was cheaper, fresher and more delicious than anyone else's.

On the other side of the square, bounded by market stalls and café tables, all kinds of performers were showing off their talents, hoping to get a few coins from the crowd. Barefoot dancers spun on the spot. Boxers jabbed and feinted, their fists wrapped in white bandages. Wrinkled old women tried to grab the hands of tourists, offering to tell their fortunes or paint their hands with henna. A band of drummers marched up and down, taking turns to drop their drum, run forward and offer a hat to onlookers, asking for a contribution.

"You want one more?" said the orange juice salesman. "I give you very good price."

Frank looked at the others. "Anyone want another?"

"We'd better get back to police station," said Harmony. "Dad might be waiting for us. He won't know where we are."

"He won't be out yet," said Ben. "That fat policeman will want to talk to them for hours."

"Then we should go home to bed."

"Why don't we wander round here first? I'd like to see the snake charmers."

"Me too," said Kitkat. "Where are they?"

"You can see them tomorrow," said Harmony.

Kitkat stamped her foot. "I want to see them now!"

"Come on, Kitkat. Don't be such a baby. You've had your drink. Now let's go back and wait for Dad."

"You do what you want," said Kitkat. "I'm going to look at the snake charmers."

She turned her back on her siblings and marched across the square, heading for the centre of the crowd.

Harmony hurried after her. "Kitkat! Kitkat! Come back here!"

Frank thanked the orange juice salesman once again, and then he and Ben sauntered after their sisters.

Ben said, "How did you know how to do that?"

"Do what?"

"Bargain with the guy selling orange juice."

"From India, I guess," said Frank. "When I went there with my mum. It's just like this. They think you must be rich because you're a tourist, so they double their prices. Or quadruple them. You have to bargain for everything."

"How do you know the right price?"

"You don't. You just offer what you want to pay. If they want to take it, they take it."

"What if they don't?"

"Then you go somewhere else."

When Ben and Frank caught up with Kitkat and Harmony, they were watching an old man with a ragged grey beard. He was squatting cross-legged on a rush mat and playing a tune on a crooked pipe, tempting a sinuous black cobra out of its wicker basket.

A beggar sat patiently on the tarmac, her skinny

arm outstretched, waiting for people to drop coins in her open palm.

A man in a blue tunic ran up to unsuspecting tourists and planted a scrawny brown monkey on their shoulders, then invited them to take photos of themselves, asking for nothing but a few dirhams in exchange.

The monkey had a frayed string collar, a bandaged paw and an expression of profound gloom.

Ben stared into the monkey's damp eyes and remembered another monkey, the strawberry thief, and how he had swung through the trees like a happy acrobat, his arms and legs reaching for the branches, every nerve in his body celebrating his freedom.

Ben wished he was rich. He would buy this monkey from its owner, take it out of the city, cut off its collar and let it loose in the jungle.

But he had no money and no way to help this sad, sorry, enslaved animal. He turned away, not wanting to watch any more.

Nearby, a crowd had gathered in a circle to watch a fight. Two men were attacking a boy. In the gloom, it was difficult to see who was winning and even whether this was an official boxing match or just an impromptu brawl between some adults and a child.

Ben and Frank moved closer to get a better look, standing on tiptoes and peering over other people's shoulders.

The combatants were unfairly matched, not just in their numbers – two against one – but their sizes too. The adults were tall and muscular. The child wasn't much more than half their height and he was skinny too. His thin cotton trousers and hoodie offered no protection against their kicks and punches. He dodged back and forth, trying to avoid the worst of their blows, but his knuckles were already bruised and a line of blood was trickling down his forehead.

The crowd had taken the boy's side. Everyone loves a loser and it was obvious that the boy was going to lose. The only question was how long he could last.

Onlookers cheered and applauded as the boy ducked punches and jumped aside to avoid kicks. But no one stepped forward to help him and no one protested at the fact that a small, skinny boy was being kicked and punched by two fully grown adults.

People must have assumed that they were

watching a performance rather than a real fight. Every night, there were several boxing matches in the Jemma al Fna, staged for the entertainment of tourists and locals. When the fight was finished and the victor has been declared, the boy and the two men would probably walk round the crowd with begging bowls, asking for coins.

Ben had been watching the fight for a minute or two before he realized that the boy was Tariq.

12

Ben yelled at Frank, telling him what he had seen. Frank responded with a question which Ben didn't hear. He was already pushing through the crowd, trying to get to the front. He tried to remember some useful French words. "*Excusez-moi. Pardon, monsieur. Pardon, madame. Je suis desolé.*"

No one liked being pushed aside. People grumbled and complained. They were watching the fight and they didn't want their view blocked.

Some of the onlookers were Moroccans. Others were tourists, snapping photos or making movies to show the folks back home. No one seemed to be sure if they were watching a boxing match or a real fight, but that was part of the fun. A performance is always more exciting if you think it might be real.

When Ben reached the front of the crowd, he stepped into the ring with both his hands raised and said in a loud, clear voice: "Stop!"

There was a moment of silence.

People stared at Ben, wondering why he had interrupted the fight. Was he another actor? Did this foreign boy have a role to play? Or was he just trying to spoil their evening?

One of the men saw his chance. He darted forward and grabbed Tariq with both hands.

Tariq struggled desperately, but the man was stronger than him.

The second man was holding a wooden box in his left hand, but his right was free. He stepped forward and slapped Tariq's face.

The noise spurred Ben into action. He charged into the centre of the ring, running straight at the two men, and yelled, "Let him go!"

Frank was less impetuous than Ben. He would have preferred to watch from the sidelines, then choose a cunning moment to intervene. But he could see he didn't have a choice. He ran forward too, hurling himself at the man who was holding Tariq, and knocked him off-balance.

The man released Tariq and whirled round, fists raised.

Frank sprang backwards.

Someone whistled. Someone cheered. Cameras focused on Frank, Ben and the two men. The crowd was getting excited. People applauded and shouted encouragement. This was what they wanted. A good fight, a fair fight, three boys against two men, the promise of some real action.

To their disappointment, nothing happened.

No one moved.

The men stared at the boys and the boys stared back again.

Each of them was waiting for someone else to take the first step, throw the first punch, ask the first question.

Tariq realized that he had been forgotten. No one was watching him. This was his chance. He twisted round, darted away and wriggled through the crowd. Ben and Frank didn't even notice him leaving, but Kitkat was more observant. She shrieked: "HE'S GETTING AWAY!"

Ben and Frank turned round, saw what was happening and sped after him.

Harmony and Kitkat sprinted round the edge of the crowd to join them.

The two men conferred for a moment.

They could have run after Ben and fought him – and Frank and Tariq and Kitkat too – and easily beaten all of them. Five kids wouldn't have a hope against two such strong, skilled fighters. And if all five of the kids had been Moroccans, that is exactly what they would have done. But there are special rules in Marrakech protecting foreigners. Robbing a tourist – or chasing him across the Jemma al Fna – will immediately attract the attention of the plain-clothes policemen who mingle with crowds, hunting pickpockets and dispersing troublemakers.

The two men turned and walked in the opposite direction. They had no desire to get the police involved in their business.

The fight over, the crowd melted away, searching for more entertainment. They didn't have to go far. There was always something to see in the Jemma al Fna – a snake or a monkey, a singer or a storyteller, a troupe of acrobats or another boxing match.

Tariq crashed through a group of Japanese tourists, scattering them in every direction, cameras swinging, arms flailing.

He pushed aside a beggar, knocked over a crate of tangerines and shoulder-barged a man on a bicycle, leaving a trail of angry words, shaken fists and squashed fruit. He put his head down and sprinted towards the edge of the square, seeking the shelter of the souk and its shadowy alleyways.

Then two men stepped forward and grabbed his arms.

Tariq struggled desperately, trying to get free, but the men were too strong for him. He slumped, despairing, accepting that he couldn't escape. As the four foreign children caught up with him and crowded round, he didn't even lift his eyes to look at them.

The two men were plain-clothes policemen.

They had been watching the boy as he sprinted across the square, pursued by four young tourists, and assumed he must be a pickpocket.

One of them jerked Tariq's arms behind his back and the other interrogated Ben, Harmony, Frank and Kitkat, asking what this boy had done to them.

13

Inspector Mahmoud took a long, hard look at Tariq. Then he turned to Robert and Celia. "This is the boy who stole your ring?"

Celia nodded. "That's him."

"You are quite sure?"

"One hundred per cent certain. I'd know him anywhere."

"Very good." Inspector Mahmoud nodded to the two plain-clothes policemen, who were still holding Tariq in a tight grip. They had marched him into the police station and summoned the inspector from his office, explaining that they had a prisoner who he would want to meet.

The policemen released their captive. Tariq didn't try to run. There was no point. Too many bodies blocked his escape routes. He'd be flattened before he got anywhere near the door.

Inspector Mahmoud stepped forward. He was a big man in every way and he towered over the small, skinny boy, his bulky body hiding the light. He barked a series of questions. Tariq offered some tentative responses. They spoke in Arabic, so no one else could understand what was said, but everyone could see that Tariq's answers failed to satisfy the inspector.

When Inspector Mahmoud had heard enough, he translated what Tariq had said. "He tells he is a guide, but not a thief. He tells he guided you to the Riad Gazelle, but he does not know nothing about your ring."

"He's lying," said Celia. "He must be."

"You are certain?"

Celia nodded. "No one else could have done it. He has to be the thief."

"I don't steal nothing," protested Tariq, his face a picture of innocence.

Inspector Mahmoud snapped at him in Arabic.

Tariq's head dropped, all defiance gone, and he stared at the floor.

Inspector Mahmoud snarled an order to his two plain-clothes policemen. One grabbed Tariq's elbows, jerking his arms behind his back and holding him still, and the other turned out his pockets, finding a few coins, a piece of string and a handful of pistachio nuts.

They checked his sandals and the seams of his clothes, then poked their fingers in his ears and forced him to open his mouth. One of the policemen ran his fingers under Tariq's tongue and round his gums.

They found nothing.

Inspector Mahmoud ordered his men to release Tariq. Then he quizzed the boy again himself.

This time, Tariq answered with nothing more than a despairing shrug of his shoulders.

That was a mistake. Inspector Mahmoud had run out of patience. He flung back his right arm and delivered a fierce, fast slap to Tariq's face.

Kitkat screamed. Harmony gasped. Ben started protesting. Celia held her hand to her mouth.

Tariq stumbled backwards, clutching his face, and fell awkwardly against the wooden bench. His legs gave way and he sprawled on the floor.

Harmony hurried forward to help him, but Inspector Mahmoud pulled her back. "Leave him!"

"But he's hurt," said Harmony. "He needs help."

"This is normal."

"What do you mean? What's normal about it?"

"Don't touch him. You will have infection. You understand?"

Harmony reluctantly retreated and joined her siblings. They could hardly believe what they had just witnessed.

Only Frank didn't look shocked. He was peering at Tariq's split lip with intense curiosity as if he was a scientist inspecting an unusual specimen that he had never previously encountered. He pulled out his phone and took a photo, then inspected the screen, seeing what he had captured.

Tariq squatted against the wall, staring nervously at the inspector. A line of blood dribbled from his split lip and seeped through his fingers.

Ben felt sick with guilt. What had he done? Rescued Tariq from one beating – and delivered him to another!

Following instructions from the inspector, the two policemen hauled Tariq from the floor and half carried, half dragged him to the cells.

Just before they reached the door, Tariq turned his head. His eyes met Ben's. A quick glance passed between them. Then the police jerked him down the corridor to the cells.

"Where are they taking him?" asked Celia. "Where's my ring?"

"You need to have no worry," said Inspector Mahmoud. "We will quickly discover who he works for."

"Who he works for? What do you mean?"

"These boys do not work alone. They work in a gang. In every gang, there is a leader. Not a boy, a man. We will find his name and then we will know where is your diamonds."

"What if he doesn't talk?" asked Robert. "How could anyone prove he's lying?"

"There is no need to worry," said the inspector with a self-satisfied smirk. "We will prove it."

14

Ben cleaned his teeth and stared at his reflection in the mirror.

His forehead looked red. He hadn't spent very much time in the sun today, but he had already been burnt. He'd have to wear a hat tomorrow.

He changed into his pyjamas, pulled back the quilt and got into bed. He switched off the light and lay on his back, staring into the darkness. He was exhausted, but he couldn't sleep. Too many questions were crowding into his mind, demanding answers. He wanted to make sense of the evening's events.

How do you steal a diamond ring?

How do you pull it from a woman's finger without her noticing?

You would need to be strong and subtle at the same time. If Tariq had really stolen the ring, he would have to be a skilled pickpocket, a brilliant burglar. Just as a magician produces a rabbit from a top hat or makes a coin disappear into a handkerchief, he had tugged a silver ring from Celia's finger without her even noticing.

Ben remembered the last glance that had passed between them, the reproachful expression in Tariq's eyes. That wasn't a look of guilt. No, not at all. That was the look of a boy who had been wrongfully accused – and wrongfully imprisoned.

What if Tariq was telling the truth? What if he was innocent? What if the whole thing had been an appalling mistake?

That made much more sense. Tariq hadn't looked or behaved like a thief. Celia had accused him without thinking through the evidence. He was the wrong boy in the wrong place at the wrong time.

Which left one question.

If Tariq wasn't the thief, then who was?

Ben thought through the events of the past few hours. He remembered looking at the ring in the restaurant, walking home, getting lost, meeting Tariq and arriving back at the Riad Gazelle. Celia said goodnight and retreated to her room. A few minutes later, she had noticed the disappearance of her diamonds and screamed so loudly that everyone came running.

During that time, who had touched Celia's left hand? Who could have slithered a silver ring from her slim finger without her noticing?

He remembered Celia offering the ring to Kitkat and Harmony in the restaurant, and them passing it to him, and him handing it back to Celia.

He went through the other people in the restaurant. The waiters, the diners, the musicians, the belly dancer. They must have noticed the three big diamonds glistening in the candlelight. Could they have sneaked across the restaurant and snatched the ring from Celia's finger?

All of them were improbable suspects, but none could be ruled out.

On their long walk from the restaurant to the riad, they had passed several more people. The tourists taking pictures, the men in the doorway, the old man in the shop, the girls with a dog. Which of them might have been the thief?

When they got back to the riad, Celia hadn't noticed the theft immediately. Someone might have been lurking in her room. But who? And how could they have escaped from the riad without being seen?

Questions, questions, questions. Filling his mind. Mingling with a mosaic of the evening's events and images. In the darkness of his imagination, he heard voices and saw snatches of action as if he was watching a movie. A dark alleyway. A boy running for his life. A snake in a wicker basket. A monkey on a chain. A belly dancer weaving between the tables. Two policemen half dragging, half carrying Tariq towards the door, taking him to the cells, and Tariq turning his head, and their eyes meeting, just for a moment.

That was the image which stayed with Ben as he drifted into a deep sleep and lingered throughout the night, surfacing in his dreams.

The expression in Tariq's eyes.

He had looked confused, desperate and frightened.

He was asking for help.

Begging for help.

15

In the morning, Robert and Celia slept late, so the others ate breakfast without them. They sat on the roof terrace, basking in the bright sunlight. Ben slapped lotion over his face, neck and arms, and wore a cap, but he was still too hot. If he didn't want to get burnt, he'd have to stay in the shade today.

The sounds of the waking city rose around them – voices, engines, a neighing donkey, cooing doves. Strange smells arrived unexpectedly on the breeze, lingered for a moment, and were whisked away. On the horizon, a shadowy line of mountains shimmered in the haze.

Mohammed brought a tray laden with tea, orange juice and croissants with jam and honey. He offered a choice of boiled eggs or scrambled. They all chose boiled.

Harmony was reading the Koran. This was her

first visit to a Muslim country, so she wanted to learn all about Islam. It was surprisingly short. She'd started on the plane and she was already halfway though.

Kitkat listened to her iPod and flicked through a couple of magazines that she'd picked up in Gatwick Airport. She pored over pictures of celebrities, inspecting their clothes, their possessions and their expressions, trying to decide what made them special. She was determined that, one day, she would be a celebrity too. She didn't care how she did it. Singing, maybe. Or acting. And if that didn't work out, she'd just have to marry a member of the royal family.

Frank fiddled with his computer. He'd probably hacked into a local network and was now checking his emails, but he might have been doing anything: writing a novel, playing a game or infiltrating the Pentagon. There was no point asking. Frank spent half his life working on his computer, but he never told anyone what he was actually doing.

Ben borrowed a pencil and a piece of paper from Harmony and made a list. Remembering what he had decided during the night, he wrote down the names of everyone who had come into contact with

Celia between arriving at La Porte d'Or and the moment that she realized the ring was missing.

WHO STOLE THE RING?
Ben
Frank
Harmony
Kitkat
Someone in the restaurant
  the waiters
  the diners
  the musicians
  the belly dancer
The old man in the carpet shop
The men in the street
The German tourists
The girls with the puppy
Mohammed

He wondered who he could cross off.

Himself, obviously.

But who else?

He was sure that the ring hadn't been stolen by Frank, Kitkat or Harmony, but he didn't have any proof of their innocence and so he felt a duty to include their names on the list. A decent detective wouldn't rule out a suspect simply because he was related to them. In fact, he could imagine good reasons why each of them might have been the thief.

Frank was always talking about the new phones and computers that he couldn't afford. A diamond ring would pay for a lot of gadgets.

Kitkat had obviously fallen in love with the ring. Maybe she couldn't resist pocketing it.

As for Harmony. . .

Anyone could see that Harmony couldn't stand Celia. She didn't want their dad to get married again. Particularly not to this skinny blonde Californian. Maybe she thought that stealing the ring would end the engagement.

Ben went through the rest of the list. None of the names struck him as likely pickpockets or burglars. And yet he couldn't rule them out.

The thief might be anyone.

Kitkat noticed that Ben was writing. He had angled his arm so no one could see the paper. She said, "What's that?"

"Nothing."

"Don't be silly. It's obviously something. Why don't you just tell me what it is?"

"It's a piece of paper."

"With what written on it?"

"Nothing."

"Stop being annoying."

"I'm not being annoying."

"Yes, you are. You've just told me you're holding *nothing* with *nothing* written on it. I'm not stupid. Are you writing a letter?"

"No."

"Are you writing to your girlfriend?"

"I don't have a girlfriend," said Ben.

"Do you have a boyfriend?"

"No."

"Then who are you writing to?"

"No one. This isn't a letter."

"Then what is it?"

Ben sighed. He could see that there would be no escape from his sister's curiosity. He reluctantly admitted that the piece of paper was a list of all the people who might have had the opportunity to take the ring from Celia's finger last night.

Kitkat was confused. "Why do you need to make a list? We caught the thief. We're just waiting for him to tell us where he hid it."

"I don't think he is the thief," said Ben.

"Why not?"

"He didn't look like a thief. Or act like a thief."

"That's true," said Kitkat. "But he did run away."

"Not from us. He was running away from those two men who were attacking him."

"Inspector Mahmoud seemed to think he was the thief."

"Maybe the inspector was wrong. The police often are. Remember what happened with Frank's mum?"

"Good point," said Kitkat.

Earlier that year, Frank's mum had gone missing. The police were useless and the Misfitz had to search for her themselves. If you want to know exactly what happened, you can read the full story in *Two Tigers on a String*.

Kitkat reached for the list. "Let me see what you've written."

"No." Ben jerked the paper away and held it out of her reach.

"Why not?"

"Because this is none of your business. Go back to reading your silly magazine."

"Let us all see," said Harmony. She had closed her book and started listening, curious to know what was going on. Even Frank had put aside his computer.

"What's going on?" said Ben. "Why are you suddenly so interested?"

"Why do you want to hide it from us?" asked Harmony.

"I'm not hiding anything. It's just private."

"What are you scared of?"

"Nothing."

"Then let us see."

Ben sighed. There was no escape. He passed the list to Harmony. She flattened it on the table. Frank and Kitkat gathered round and the three of them read the list of names.

16

Harmony straightened up and stared angrily at her younger brother. "Why am I on this list? Are you accusing *me* of stealing that stupid ring?"

Kitkat chimed in. "And me! I'm there too! He's accusing me too!"

"I'm not saying you took it," said Ben. "I'm just saying you might have."

"You're horrible," said Kitkat. "How could you think that?"

"You liked the ring, didn't you?"

"I like lots of things," said Kitkat. "But I don't steal them, do I?"

"No," said Ben. "But. . ."

"But what?"

"I wanted to put every possible suspect on this list."

"I'm not a thief," said Kitkat.

"I know you're not."

"So cross me off."

"Fine." Ben drew a line through her name.

"And me, please," said Harmony. "I didn't steal it either."

"Fine." He took her name off too.

He looked at Frank, waiting for him to demand that his name was removed, but Frank just shrugged his shoulders.

"I know I didn't steal it," said Frank. "I can't offer any evidence in my defence and so I can't prove my innocence. If you want to write down every potential suspect, you'd better leave my name on the list."

"Thank you," said Ben. He approved of Frank's logic. He wished his sisters were so sensible too.

"You've missed someone," said Harmony.

"Who?"

"I'd have thought it was pretty obvious."

"Not to me." Ben looked at the list. "You don't mean Dad, do you?"

"No."

"Then who?"

"Oh, come on. Who is the one person who had access to the ring at all times? Who could have stolen it more easily than anyone else? Who could have taken it without making any effort?"

"I don't know."

"I'm talking about the person who was wearing it."

Ben laughed. "I know you hate Celia because she's marrying Dad, but that doesn't make her a thief."

"I don't hate her."

"You don't like her, do you?"

"I don't mind her. I just think she's too young for him. He should be with a woman his own age."

"That doesn't make her a thief. Why would she want to steal her own ring?"

"Maybe she needs the money. Maybe she's a kleptomaniac. I don't know. But you should still put her on the list. She could have done it more easily than anyone else."

Kitkat said, "What's a klepto-thingy?"

"A kleptomaniac?" said Harmony.

"Exactly," said Kitkat. "What's one of them?"

"A kleptomaniac is someone who can't help stealing things. They don't even know why they're doing it. They just can't stop themselves. It's a kind of psychological problem."

Kitkat was fascinated. "You think Celia's one of them?"

"I don't know what she is," said Harmony. "Or

92

who she is. I don't know anything about her. I thought she was just another of Dad's endless supply of dim-witted, leggy blondes. And then he suddenly announced he was going to marry her. To me, the whole thing seems extremely suspicious. I'd like to know a little more about her. I wouldn't be at all surprised if she turned out to be a thief."

"Fine," said Ben. He scrawled another name on the bottom on the list. "She's on it."

"You can take off another name," said Kitkat. "Mohammed didn't do it. He didn't go anywhere near Celia."

"How do you know?" asked Ben.

"Because I was there. I saw what happened. Mohammed opened the door. We walked in. Celia went straight upstairs. He stayed with us. There wasn't a single moment when he could have touched her hand."

"Off he goes," said Ben, drawing a line through Mohammed's name.

Frank said, "You need to think carefully about what happened last night. When did each of you last see the ring? Who can remember? Anyone?"

"In the restaurant," said Kitkat.

"Me too," said Ben. "When we were looking at

it. Then I handed it back to Celia and she put it on her finger."

"I saw it once after that," said Harmony. "When Celia kneeled down to pat that puppy, she was still wearing the ring."

"Are you sure?" asked Frank.

"Yes, I saw it on her hand. I remember looking at it and thinking she should be more careful. Those girls could have stolen it. Or someone might have mugged us. Anyone could see how much that ring was worth. I remember being shocked Celia wasn't taking better care of something so valuable."

"Did anyone see it after that?" said Frank.

No one had.

Frank turned to Ben. "That was the last known sighting of the ring. You can adjust your list. Cross off everyone who came into contact with the ring before you met those girls with the puppy."

Ben did as Frank had asked and crossed off several names from the list. He drew a line through Frank's name too. Proof or no proof, he didn't believe Frank had taken it.

He placed the list on the table and turned it to face the others.

WHO STOLE THE RING?
~~Ben~~
~~Frank~~
~~Harmony~~
~~Kitkat~~
~~Someone in the restaurant~~
 ~~the waiters~~
 ~~the diners~~
 ~~the musicians~~
 ~~the belly dancer~~
~~The old man in the carpet shop~~
~~The men in the street~~
~~The German tourists~~
~~The girls with the puppy~~
~~Mohammed~~
Celia

"It's her!" yelped Kitkat. "There's no one else! It has to be her! She's a klepto-thingy!"

"I don't think so," said Harmony. "She's probably just a common thief. She took her own ring and blamed an innocent boy. She's going to sell the ring and then get Dad to buy her another."

"She's probably a murderer too," said Kitkat. "She'll marry him and make him change his will and then she'll kill him and keep all his money. I've seen it happen on TV."

Ben said, "That's why it won't happen in real life."

"It might! You should warn your dad. You should tell him to dis-engage her."

"What if he doesn't want to?" said Ben.

"You still have to tell him," insisted Kitkat. "How would you feel if she murdered him and you hadn't even tried to save him? Huh? Come on! Let's tell him now!"

"We can't," said Harmony.

"Why not?"

"Because he won't listen to us. He's been blinded by love. If we're going to save him, we have to be more subtle."

17

They heard Robert before they saw him, striding up the stairs and whistling merrily. He emerged on to the roof terrace, his hair still wet from the shower, his face beaming with a big smile. "Hey! You're all here! I'm so pleased." He quizzed them each in turn, asking whether their beds had been comfortable and their rooms quiet, before explaining that his own bed was so deliciously snug that Celia couldn't be persuaded to leave it. "But I wanted to get up and have breakfast with you guys."

"We've already had breakfast," said Kitkat.

"Have some more. You're not on a diet, are you?"

"No, but I'm full. Anyway, I have to go downstairs."

"Why?"

"I need the loo."

"If you've gotta go, you've gotta go. See you later, Kitkat. Now, where's Mohammed? I can't survive without a cup of coffee."

A moment later, Frank excused himself. Then Ben did too. Harmony had asked them to leave her alone with her father.

Mohammed brought a pot of coffee, a jug of hot milk, a glass of freshly squeezed orange juice and two warm croissants. "*Voilà, monsieur. Du café, des croissants.* You would like one boiled egg?"

"I'd like two boiled eggs," said Robert. "Four and a half minutes in the water, please. And do you have toast? You do? Excellent, I'd like two slices of wheatgerm toast with unsalted butter. Thank you very much." He rubbed his hands together and grinned at his daughter. "Isn't this perfect?"

"It's lovely."

Robert shielded his eyes against the sun's glare and stared at the distant mountains. "Tomorrow night, we'll be halfway up one of them. That's a good thought, huh?"

"Dad, can I talk to you?"

"Aren't we talking right now?"

"There's something I want to say."

"Then you must say it. Speak your mind. You know, Harmony, we don't talk nearly enough. I wish you came to Los Angeles more often. Why don't you come and do a year of high school? You could live with me and make some American friends. Wouldn't that be good?"

"I can't leave school. I've got exams."

"There are more important things in life than exams."

"Like what?"

"Like what?" Robert laughed. "Is that a serious question? You're too young to worry about exams. You should be thinking about the good things in life. Like love. And pleasure. And sunshine. And croissants. Speaking of which. . ." He grabbed a croissant from the plate and dipped its corner in his milky coffee. "Didn't you want to talk to me about something?"

"Yes, I did," said Harmony. "The thing is, Dad, it's a bit delicate."

"You want me to tell you about the birds and the bees?"

"No, thanks. Actually, it's about Celia."

"Celia? I told you, she's still in bed. But she'll be up soon. You can talk to her then."

"I don't want to talk to her. I want to talk to you about her."

"Oh, yeah? What do you want to say?"

Harmony unfolded the list of suspects and laid it on the table beside her father's cup of coffee. She led him through the names, explaining why each of them had been crossed off. There was simply no alternative, she explained. Only one person could possibly be the thief.

When she had finished, Robert threw back his head and laughed so loudly that a nearby flock of doves was shocked into flight. They wheeled through the sky and came back to roost on another rooftop.

Harmony said, "What's so funny?"

"This whole ludicrous story," said Robert. "I've never heard anything funnier in my entire life."

"Actually, it's not ludicrous. It's very serious."

"Oh, come on. It's natural you shouldn't like Celia. She's the wicked stepmother, right? I wish you did like her. And she wishes you did too. But if you don't, you don't. That's fine. Just let me ask you to do one thing, Harmony. Accept her. She's not an evil queen who'll prick your finger and send you to sleep for a hundred years. But she is a very beautiful, very intelligent and very sophisticated woman. And I happen to be marrying her. Like her or don't like her, that's your choice, but there's no need to make up these crazy stories."

Harmony took a deep breath. However much her dad irritated her, she didn't want to get cross with him. That would only backfire. She had to stay calm and make him see sense. "It's nothing to do with liking her or not liking her. I just think you should consider the possibility that she's not who she seems to be."

"Oh, yeah? And who is she?"

"I don't know. But you should be careful, Dad. What if she is the thief?"

"She's not."

"How do you know?"

"There is one pretty obvious candidate," said Robert. "Or have you forgotten him? A little boy, remember? Who we met in the street?"

Harmony shook her head. "You saw what he looked like. And how he behaved. There is no way that he was a thief."

"You may be right." Robert paused for thought, chewing on the last scraps of his croissant. "Maybe someone else stole the ring."

"Who?"

"Someone in the street. Someone in the hotel."

"Oh, Dad. Think about the timings. Celia has to be the prime suspect."

"You're wrong," said Robert. "Celia didn't take it,

I know she didn't. Now, can we change the subject? This is becoming tiresome. What do you want to do today? Shall we go sightseeing?"

Harmony sighed. She couldn't believe that her dad was so stubborn. "So that's it? You're going to leave an innocent boy to rot in prison?"

"Chill out, Harmony. You're supposed to be on holiday. Why don't you try to enjoy yourself? You take life too seriously, honey. You should learn to relax."

"That's just your problem, Dad. You're too relaxed."

"I'll take that as a compliment." Robert had finished his first croissant. He ripped a corner from the second and absent-mindedly dipped it into his orange juice. "I don't want to be rude, Harmony, but you need to be careful. You don't want to grow up into your mother. You're very like her already. Too like her, in fact. You've got some of her best qualities – and some of her worst ones too. You're inhibited. You're too analytical. You step back from life. Plunge in! The water's warm! You know, honey, you have to give yourself up to experiences. You have to welcome them. It's all a question of attitude. You're young, Harmony. There's no need to be so mature all the time. Relax. Let it all hang out.

You know what your problem is? You don't know how to enjoy yourself."

"Oh, this is ridiculous!" Harmony didn't want to hear another word of the nonsense that spilled from her father's mouth. She sprang to her feet and marched angrily across the roof terrace towards the stairs.

Her father called after her, asking her to come back, but Harmony took no notice. She strode down the stairs and went to find the others.

She couldn't believe how her father had reacted. He was so stubborn! So irritating! Such a jerk!

It was just as she'd said. He was blinded by love. A wicked woman had duped him, pulling the wool over his eyes, and he couldn't see what was right in front of him.

18

A friend of a friend of a friend of Robert's worked at the American Embassy in Casablanca. When he heard about the robbery, he was very sympathetic, but not surprised. Marrakech is full of thieves, he told Robert. If you don't know the city, you shouldn't walk through the streets at night without a guide. He recommended an English-speaking lawyer who would be able to help in their dealings with the police.

Mohammed summoned a taxi to take Robert and Celia to the lawyer's office. Robert told Mohammed to keep a close watch on the children. "Whatever you do, don't let them leave the riad. Do you understand what I'm saying? They don't walk out of this door. I always thought Jennifer was being melodramatic, but now I know what she was talking about. Leave them alone for a second and they'll vanish."

"Jennifer?" asked Mohammed. "Who is Jennifer?"

"Forget it. Just keep an eye on the kids. When I come back, I want to find them right here where I left them. Do you understand?"

"No problem," said Mohammed. "They will stay here."

Robert said goodbye to the children. "We're going to talk through our options with a lawyer and then we'll come right back. We'll be an hour, maybe two. You can look after yourselves, can't you?"

"Of course we can," said Harmony. "We look after ourselves all the time."

They sat on the roof terrace, waiting for their father and his girlfriend to go out. They could hear the noises of departure rising up from the floors below: Celia's high-pitched voice, Robert's response, footsteps on the stairs and a door slamming.

They waited for five minutes. Just in case Robert had forgotten something and doubled back to pick it up.

When the five minutes were up, Ben peered over the balcony.

He couldn't see Mohammed, but he could hear voices from the ground floor. He listened for a moment, trying to work out what they were saying. Then he realized Mohammed was watching TV.

He nodded to the others. They tiptoed through the riad in single file. Down the stairs from the roof terrace to the first floor. Along the gallery to the master suite.

Ben knocked on the door.

He wanted to check no one was inside. A housemaid might be cleaning the room. Or Celia could have changed her mind and stayed behind. But there was no answer.

He knocked once more, just to make sure, then turned the handle.

In an ordinary hotel, rooms have locks, but riads are different. You hire the whole place, so there's no need to secure the doors. If you're worried about any of your valuables, you can lock them in a safe in your room.

Ben stood on the threshold for a few moments, staring at the clothes strewn on the bed, the suitcases on the floor, the books on the bedside tables. The others were waiting behind him, but they didn't urge him forward.

"This feels weird," whispered Kitkat.

"That's because it is weird," whispered Frank. "What are we going to say if we get caught?"

"It'll be fine," said Harmony. "Frank, Kitkat, you're on guard duty. Ben, come with me." She pushed past her brother and marched into the room.

Frank went downstairs to the courtyard and sat in a wicker chair by the fountain. He opened his computer on his knees, set out the pieces on the chessboard and moved them occasionally, just to give the impression that he was working through the moves of a game. But his attention was really focused on the front door, waiting to see if anyone came in.

Kitkat lingered at the top of the stairs. If Frank signalled to her, or if she saw anyone herself, she would sprint into the master suite and fetch the others.

Ben and Harmony stepped nervously over the threshold. They didn't know their father very well. They hadn't lived with him since they were tiny and now never saw him for more than a couple of weeks each year. Peering at his things, they felt like spies.

Ben said, "Do you want to take the bathroom or the bedroom?"

"You can do the bathroom. I'll stay in here."

Ben went into the bathroom. He searched in the

shower and peered behind the toilet. He shook out the towels, opened the washbags, inspected the pill bottles, unwound the lipsticks, sniffed the perfumes, emptied the toothbrush holder and removed the tops from Celia's shampoos. He found a plastic box packed with a mass of jewellery – earrings, necklaces, brooches, bangles and rings of all colours, shapes and designs – but not a shiny silver ring encrusted with three large diamonds.

Harmony left the bed till last. She hunted through everything else in the room: the expensive leather suitcases, the tall wooden cupboards, the sofa, the chairs, the desk and the bedside tables. She ruffled through the pages of the books on the shelves, then checked the pockets of Celia's and Robert's clothes. She found some dollars and some dirhams, a little black notebook, a silver pencil, several receipts, the stubs of plane tickets, a pebble, a tiny tub of lip balm, a champagne cork and a map of Marrakech, but no ring.

There was only one place left to look.

Ben and Harmony stood at the end of the immense bed. It was big enough for an entire family.

Harmony picked up the pillows and shook them out, then pulled back the sheets, but she couldn't see any sign of the ring.

Ben knelt on the floor and peered under the bed. His eyes took a few seconds to adjust to the darkness. He lay down and pushed himself into the narrow gap between the floorboards and the bottom of the bed. He was just small enough to squeeze through. Anyone bigger than him would have got stuck immediately.

The bulky mattress and the bedboards were pressing down on his spine. The darkness surrounded him. Dust tickled his nostrils.

Up ahead, he could see a small, shiny object lodged between two floorboards. He pushed and squeezed and shoved, then stretched out his right arm, opened his fingers and grabbed it, whatever it was.

Gripping the object tightly in his fist, he wriggled backwards, eased himself out of the bed and stood up.

When Ben opened his fist, he felt a quick jolt of disappointment. He'd found a plastic lighter decorated with a picture of a camel. Neither Robert nor Celia smoked, so it must have been dropped by a previous guest. He dropped the lighter in his pocket, then nodded to Harmony. They looked around the room, making sure they had left no sign of their presence, and tiptoed out.

19

Kitkat stamped her foot. "This is hopeless! It's so unfair! Tariq is going to spend the rest of his life in prison for a crime he didn't commit."

"You don't have to worry about Tariq," said Harmony. "If he's innocent, he'll be released. Dad is the one who's going to get a life sentence."

Frank said, "I don't share your confidence in the Moroccan legal system. It's quite possible that innocence offers no guarantees."

"Translation, please?" asked Kitkat.

"Being innocent won't help Tariq," explained Frank. "I think they'll torture him. They'll carry on torturing him till he confesses. A confession would allow them to keep him in prison for years."

Ben said, "Why would he confess if he's innocent?"

"That's what people do when they're tortured. They'll say anything to stop the pain. Which is why most government agencies don't actually consider torture to be a very valuable device for gathering accurate information."

Kitkat said, "What will they do to him?"

"Oh, just the usual stuff," said Frank. "Sleep deprivation. Water-boarding. Stubbing out cigarettes on the soles of his feet."

"That's disgusting!" Kitkat covered her eyes. Then she took her hands away and glared furiously at the others. "We've got to do something! We've got to help him!"

"What can we do?" said Frank.

"I don't know. Something!"

Frank shook his head. "I can't think of a single thing that we could do."

"Let's tell them about Celia," suggested Harmony.

"What can we tell them? We don't have any evidence. It's her word against his. Given the choice between a rich American tourist and a skinny kid from the slums, who are the police going to believe?"

"Then we have to find some evidence against her," said Kitkat.

"Like what?"

"Like, um. . ." Kitkat bit her lip. She pulled the

list towards her and stared at the names of the other suspects, but they didn't offer any inspiration. She sighed despondently and put her head in her hands.

The sun was higher now and hotter too, casting a brutal white light over the roofs of Marrakech. A single stork wheeled overhead in the clear blue sky. Swallows swooped across the roofs, darting through the forest of TV aerials.

Ben stared at the city and wondered why he had been such an idiot.

It was his fault. He'd seen Tariq fighting those two men. He'd jumped into the fight. And, worst of all, he'd chased Tariq though the square, driving him towards the two plain-clothes policemen.

If he hadn't interfered, Tariq would still be free.

Now Tariq was trapped in a prison cell. Frank was probably right: the police would torture him till he confessed. Desperate to stop the pain, Tariq would tell them whatever they wanted to hear. And he'd be stuck in there for years.

It's my fault, thought Ben.

I put him there. And now I can't help him.

Unless. . .

"I've got an idea," said Ben. He waited till he had

the full attention of the others and then he explained. "We can't find the ring. We can't prove Celia stole it. She's probably hidden it so well that we'd never be able to find it. But we could do something else instead. We put Tariq in prison. If we hadn't interfered, he'd still be free. I think we should get him out again."

"That's a good idea," said Kitkat, suddenly excited again. "Then he could help us find the real thief."

"We know who the thief is," said Harmony.

"We're not sure it's her," said Ben.

"I'm sure."

"You don't have any proof."

"I don't need proof. I know I'm right."

"We can talk about this later," said Ben, not wanting to get involved in an endless argument with his stubborn sister. "The point is, are we going to break Tariq out of prison?"

"Definitely," said Kitkat.

"I suppose it's worth trying," said Harmony.

"There's only one problem," said Frank. "Tariq is locked in a cell in the middle of a police station. There'll be a guard outside. More police everywhere else. And several more locked doors between the cell and the exit. Even if we got in, which is extremely unlikely, there is absolutely no way we could get him out again."

"Don't be such a pessimist," said Ben. "We could do it."

"How?"

20

Harmony was the oldest, and therefore the most likely to be trusted, so she went downstairs and talked to Mohammed.

He was sitting in the reception area, watching a football match on a small television. He listened to Harmony politely and respectfully, but refused to open the front door for her. He had been instructed to keep the four children inside the riad and he wasn't going to let them overrule their father.

Harmony returned to the terrace and told the others what Mohammed had said. Their plan had failed at the first attempt.

Ben sighed. "We're stuck. It's hopeless."

"I don't want to be rude," said Frank. "But I knew your plan wouldn't work."

Ben didn't reply. He felt too depressed. He'd come up with a brilliant plan, but they couldn't do anything, because they were trapped inside this stupid riad.

What could they do?

Sneak past Mohammed while he wasn't looking?

No, that just wasn't possible. He was sitting right next to the front door. And even when he went to the loo or fetched a glass of water, he'd probably lock the door with a key. They'd never be able to get out.

"There is one thing we could do," said Kitkat.

"Oh yeah? What?"

"Climb over the roof."

"Which roof?"

"This roof," said Kitkat. "We could climb over the edge of the roof, jump across the gap and get into the next building."

"How are we supposed to do that?"

"With that ladder."

While they had been sitting on the roof terrace, Kitkat had noticed a long wooden ladder lying against one of the walls.

Ben sprang to his feet and hurried across the terrace. The others followed him. They examined the ladder. It looked ancient and rickety. The wooden rungs were held in place with rusty old nails. But when Ben shook it, the ladder felt reasonably secure. If they were lucky, it would hold their weight.

Ben and Frank carefully lifted up the ladder, carried it across the terrace and laid it over the narrow gap that divided the Riad Gazelle from the next building in the street.

"That looks dangerous," said Harmony.

"It'll be fine," said Ben, trying to sound more confident than he actually felt.

"Are you sure?"

"Of course I am." Ben grinned. He hated heights, but he didn't want anyone to know that. Anyway, he was sure he would be fine. He just had to stop himself looking down. "I'll go first."

Ben placed his hands on the end of the ladder.

The wobbly wooden rungs looked as if they might give way at any moment, but Ben didn't want to show any fear. He put his full weight on the ladder and crawled slowly across the bridge between the two buildings.

Don't look down, he told himself. Don't look down. Whatever you do, you must not look down.

But he couldn't help it. He looked down.

And immediately regretted it.

Below him, he could see a dizzyingly long drop to the ground, twenty or thirty metres below him.

If he fell, he'd land with a bang and break every bone in his body.

His hands were starting to sweat. He wanted to hurl himself forward and throw himself across to the other side. But he forced himself to crawl slowly and carefully from rung to rung, his hands keeping a tight grip on the wooden ladder.

Then he was on the other side. He stepped down and waved at the others. His feet felt wobbly. "No problem," he called across the gap. "It's easy. Come on! Who's next?"

"Me," said Kitkat. She was smaller and lighter than Ben, and maybe she was braver too, because she scurried across the ladder as if she was simply crawling across the floor.

Harmony was the opposite. She took at least a minute to inch her way across the ladder, stopping constantly, staring down at the ground as if she had never seen anything so horrifying.

"Don't look," said Ben. "Just lift up your head and keep moving."

"I know," whispered Harmony. She shuffled forward, then stared down, down, down at the ground, imagining herself toppling through the air and crashing in the dust.

When she finally reached the end of the ladder,

she rolled off and squatted on the floor, drawing deep breaths into her lungs. "Never again," she whispered. "Never again. I didn't know I was so scared of heights."

Now it was Frank's turn.

He was holding his computer in both hands.

He didn't know what to do.

He knew he couldn't crawl across the ladder with his computer. But he didn't want to leave it behind. His computer was his constant companion, his best friend, half his brain. He couldn't go anywhere without it.

He could have thrown it across the gap to Ben or Harmony, but he didn't want to risk them dropping it.

He realized he had a simple choice. He could either join the others and break Tariq out of prison. Or he could stay here with his computer.

"I'll be back in a minute," he said.

He ran downstairs to his bedroom and hid his computer in the cupboard. Then he returned to the roof terrace and crawled across the ladder. Just like Kitkat, he didn't show a trace of nervousness. He scurried over the rungs, sprang off the end and looked around. "This is nice."

"Where are we?" whispered Kitkat.

"On top of someone's house," said Ben. "Or another hotel."

They were standing on the roof terrace of another riad very much like the one where they were staying. There were cushions, tables and chairs, and a big awning to provide some shade from the sun.

"We're trespassing," said Harmony. "If we get caught, we'll be in serious trouble."

"That would be perfect," said Kitkat. "We'll get sent to prison. Then we'd definitely see Tariq."

"It wouldn't be perfect at all," said Frank. "Let's get out of here."

They hurried across the roof terrace and walked down the stairs. They went down one flight, then another, and then they met a housemaid coming the other way. When she saw them, she dropped her mop and let out a high-pitched shriek of terror.

Harmony hurried forward, speaking in French, trying to placate her. "*Pardon, madame. Nous ne sommes pas des voleurs. Nous sommes perdues.*"

After a quick discussion, the housemaid decided that Harmony was harmless. She led them down the rest of the stairs, ushered them outside and bolted the front door after them. They were standing in the street, one door down from the Riad Gazelle.

"Hey, Harmony, that was cool," said Kitkat. "How come you speak such good French?"

"I learn it at school."

"So does Ben and he can't speak it at all."

Harmony smiled smugly. "That's because I concentrate in lessons and he just stares out of the window."

Ben couldn't deny it. He had sat through endless French classes at school, but he couldn't say more than a few simple sentences. *"Bonjour, je m'appelle Ben. J'habites à Londres. J'aimes les pommes de terres. Je detestes le brocoli."* He'd never seen the point of listening to his French teacher, Monsieur Leconte, because he had never wanted to go to France. If he'd known that you could use the same language to speak to Africans, he might have taken more notice.

"Let's get going," said Frank. "We don't want Mohammed to see us. And your dad might come back any minute now."

Harmony said, "Which way is the Jemma al Fna?"

"The what?" said Kitkat.

"The big square."

"This way," said Ben, taking a couple of paces down the alley.

Kitkat said, "How do you know?"

"I've got a photographic memory."

"No, you haven't."

"You're right," said Ben. "But I do remember the route. We've walked it several times now."

The others didn't have any better ideas, so they followed Ben through the narrow streets.

He led them left and right and left again, past a few landmarks that he recognized: a signpost to the Hotel Safari, a kiosk selling cigarettes and fruit, a small door marked ACCESS INTERDIT.

He thought he was going in the right direction, but he couldn't be sure. He hoped he wasn't making a fool of himself. He didn't want to be like his dad.

They reached a crossroads. Ben paused for a second, wondering whether to go left or right. He didn't have a clue. Both directions looked the same. Not wanting to admit that he was lost, he simply turned left and walked briskly along the alleyway. The others followed him without question.

They squeezed past a donkey and cart, avoided a beggar's outstretched hand, ignored the pleas of a carpet salesman and emerged into the noise and bustle and chaos and confusion of the Jemma al Fna.

"You're a genius," said Kitkat.

"Thanks," said Ben, hoping she couldn't see how relieved he was feeling.

The square looked different in daylight. Street cleaners were washing the tarmac. A few customers were sitting at café tables, sipping glasses of milky coffee. Last night's frantic crowd had gone, replaced by a couple of snake charmers, some drummers and a man with a monkey on his shoulder. He made a dash for the Misfitz, hoping to beg some coins, but they dodged past him and headed for the police station.

21

A uniformed officer was sitting behind the main desk. *"Oui? Puis-je vous aider? Mademoiselle?"*

Harmony walked straight past as if she hadn't heard him and headed down the corridor. The others hurried after her.

The policeman sprang up from his desk and yelled after them. *"Heh! Les enfants! Revenez ici!"*

But they had already gone.

The policeman hesitated. He was alone and he couldn't leave his desk. He looked around hoping one of his colleagues might have heard his shouting and come to investigate, but no one appeared. He sighed, sat down and returned to his paperwork.

They walked down one corridor, then another, and then Harmony stopped and peered at her surroundings with a puzzled expression. "I think I'm lost."

"Follow me," said Ben.

He led the way to the inspector's office. He remembered the route from last time.

The door was closed.

Harmony knocked twice. There was no answer. She knocked again, louder. A voice came from the other side. They didn't know whether the inspector was telling them to come in or go away, but Harmony opened the door anyway and they walked into the office.

Inspector Mahmoud was sitting behind his desk, talking on the phone. He covered the receiver with his right hand. "Please, you will wait outside."

Harmony said, "*Excusez-moi, Inspector Mahmoud, mais je veux vous parler d'un sujet de grande importance.*"

"*Vous parlez français?*"

"*Oui, un peu.*"

"*Un moment.*" The inspector put the phone to his ear, talked for a few moments in Arabic, then ended the call. He invited Harmony to sit down and started quizzing her in French, asking what she wanted.

The others couldn't follow the conversation, so they stood in silence, wondering what their sister and the inspector were talking about.

Eventually, Harmony explained. "The inspector has agreed with our plan. He thinks we might be right. Maybe Tariq will talk to us because we're children too. So he's going to let us see him on our own. He's doing us a special favour. You're not normally allowed to see prisoners in their cells unless you're a lawyer. So be nice."

Ben, Frank and Kitkat didn't need prompting. They had already rehearsed what to say. "*Merci, monsieur. Merci beaucoup. Vous êtes très gentil.*"

A uniformed policeman escorted them down a flight of stairs and through a series of dingy, windowless corridors. They came to a line of doors with little peepholes, allowing guards to spy on the prisoners.

The policeman unlocked the cell and ushered them inside. When they were finished, he said, they should knock on the door and ask to be released. He would be waiting outside. He closed the door and they heard the click-clunk of the key in the lock.

The cell was a small, low-ceilinged room with whitewashed walls and no window. The only light came from a single bare bulb. There was an old wooden chair, a small bed with a skinny mattress and a bucket for a toilet.

Tariq was sitting on the bed. He stared at them suspiciously. "Yes? What do you do here?"

"We've come to rescue you," whispered Kitkat.

"*Rescue*? What is *rescue*?"

"Shh!" Kitkat put her finger to her lips, then glanced at the door. The peephole remained closed and the guard made no noise. Nevertheless, Kitkat spoke in a whisper, barely loud enough for Tariq to hear. "We're going to get you out of here."

"You got me in," said Tariq. "Why you get me out?"

"Because we made a mistake," said Harmony. "We're sorry. We should never have brought you here. And now we're going to make it right."

"But you have to do something for us in exchange," said Ben. "If we get you out of prison, will you help us find the real thief?"

"What thief?" asked Tariq.

"The person who stole the diamonds."

Tariq thought for a moment. Then he nodded. "Yes, it is fair."

"You'll find him?" asked Ben.

"Her," added Harmony.

"I will find him," promised Tariq.

He shook hands with each of them to seal the

bargain. He couldn't give them any more than a handshake, but that was enough. They trusted him.

"So," whispered Tariq. "How you get me out?"

Ben explained his plan.

At first, Tariq thought it was a joke. Then he looked at their four solemn faces and realized they were serious. He glanced shyly at Harmony. "You will do this thing for me?"

"I will," said Harmony.

"Thank you. A thousand times, I say thank you."

"You don't have to thank me," said Harmony. "You just have to help us find the thief – and get those diamonds back."

"Like I said, I will find him."

Harmony unwrapped the scarf that she was wearing around her head. "Can you turn around? Not you, Kitkat. Just the boys. All three of you. Face the wall, please."

Ben, Frank and Tariq did as she asked. They turned their backs on Harmony and stared at the blank white wall.

Harmony wriggled out of her long skirt and her cotton shirt. She handed them to Kitkat. "Give those to Tariq, please."

Kitkat carried the clothes across the cell.

Tariq took off his trousers, his hoodie and his shirt. He was wearing nothing but a pair of grubby underpants, but he wasn't embarrassed. He didn't care if other people saw his skinny body. He gave his clothes to Kitkat and took Harmony's skirt and blouse in exchange.

For Harmony, there was nothing unusual about wearing trousers and a hoodie, and she didn't feel at all embarrassed. She hitched up the trousers and lifted the hoodie, hiding her face.

Tariq had never worn women's clothes before. He self-consciously smoothed the long skirt over his hips and blushed bright pink. Then he wrapped the scarf around his face, hiding every part of himself except his eyes.

The policeman was bored.

He hoped those kids wouldn't be long.

He didn't know why they wanted to talk to the pickpocket and he didn't really care. He had more important things to worry about. Like his stomach, for instance. And when he might be able to fill it.

He wandered up and down the corridor, whistling tunelessly and dreaming about lunch. Breakfast had been hours ago and he hadn't had a moment to stop for his usual coffee and pastry. All he wanted was a cheese sandwich. Or a bowl of soup. Or both.

When he finally heard a shout from the cell, he hurried forward and unlocked the door. The four children filed out – the two boys, the young girl and the older girl with a scarf wrapped around her head.

The policeman hardly glanced at them, just slammed the door and locked it, then hurried them towards the exit, eager to get rid of them as quickly as possible.

22

Harmony listened to their footsteps retreating down the corridor.

A door creaked open and slammed shut. Then they were gone.

She was alone.

She squatted on the bed, her back against the wall, her knees drawn up to her chest, her hands wrapped round her knees. The hoodie was up. She hoped her face couldn't be seen by a guard peering through the peephole.

She looked around the cell. Her home for the next few hours.

Cells in movies often have windows, but this one just had four blank walls, a grubby floor and a low ceiling. Nothing to look at. Nothing to do. Nowhere to go except the other end of the cell, and that wasn't more than five paces away.

Some graffiti had been scrawled on the wall, but

she couldn't decipher the Arabic letters. She wondered who had been here before her and what crimes they had committed. Who had sat on this bed? Who had peed in that bucket? Thieves? Murderers? She shivered. This was the first time that she had ever been in prison and she hoped it would be the last.

She wondered how long she would have to stay here.

When she agreed to Kitkat's plan, she hadn't given much thought to the time that she would actually spend in prison. She hadn't wondered how she would feel, stuck in a small cell, or what she would actually do to use up the time. How was she going to fill the next few hours?

She should have brought a book.

On second thought: no, she shouldn't. Tariq probably couldn't read, so the guards would be very suspicious if they saw him hunched over a book. They'd charge into the cell and snatch the book from his hands and pull the hoodie from his face and. . .

She would be caught eventually. Of course she would. A guard would shout a question at her and she wouldn't be able to answer. Or the inspector would come down to the cells to interrogate Tariq.

She just hoped it didn't happen soon. The others needed a few hours. Long enough to find the ring – or the evidence to prove that Celia had stolen it.

23

Inspector Mahmoud was leaning against the counter in the main lobby. When he saw the four children, he gulped down the last scraps of a pastry, licked the sugar from his fingers and smiled. "*Ah, les enfants! Avez-vous éclairci l'affaire des diamants perdus?*"

He was obviously expecting Harmony to reply to him in French, but the girl kept quiet, her face hidden behind a long scarf, her head turned slightly as if she had seen something fascinating at the other end of the room. She hurried past him, heading for the door.

Ben let Frank and Kitkat follow Tariq out of the police station while he stayed behind to distract Inspector Mahmoud. He said, "I'm afraid we didn't have any success."

"He did talk?" asked the inspector.

"No."

"You find the diamonds?"

"No." Ben tried to look humble. "We thought we could do better than the police, but we were wrong. So we've decided to leave it to the professionals. This is your job, not ours."

Inspector Mahmoud chuckled. "You are young, but you are very wise."

"Thank you," said Ben. "If you don't mind, I should go now. Our father will be waiting for me."

"Yes, yes. You must go. But first, I must ask you one question." Inspector Mahmoud reached for the plate of pastries. "Here is a speciality of our country. You will have one?"

Ben thanked him and explained that he'd just eaten breakfast. The inspector shrugged his shoulders, popped another pastry in his own mouth and wished him a good day. Then he turned his back on Ben and chatted to the policeman behind the desk.

Ben wanted to run, but he knew it would look suspicious, so he strolled slowly out of the door and searched for the others. The sunlight blinded him for a moment; then he saw them, waiting for him in the shadows of a side street.

*

Kitkat suggested returning to the stalls in the Jemma al Fna and buying some more glasses of orange juice, but Tariq knew somewhere better.

"For tourists," he said about the stalls. "Too much big price. I will take you to a good place. Come, this way."

He led them into the souk.

Noise and bustle surrounded them. Salesmen lurched forward, offering carpets and slippers. Stalls offered spices and olives and CDs and knickers and anything else that you might want to buy. A blind beggar jangled a few coins in a battered tin cup. Twenty chickens squawked in cages. If you wanted one for your supper, you had to take it home and kill it yourself.

Tariq could easily have slipped away, dodging down an alleyway or disappearing into the crowd, and they never would have found him, but he kept his word. He had promised to help them and so he would.

He took them to a small café. The entrance was an unmarked doorway shrouded by a thick, dusty curtain. You wouldn't have known that you were stepping into a café rather than a private house. It was the type of place that foreigners would never venture into.

Inside, the grey walls were lit by a single bare bulb. The only other customer was a black cat, snoozing in the corner, but the tables were clean, the chairs were comfortable and the proprietor, a fat woman with a white apron and a beaming smile, served them tall glasses of fresh orange juice for only two dirhams each.

Frank thought about bargaining, but decided not to bother. If you went to a café at home, two dirhams wouldn't even buy a sip of orange juice, let alone a whole glass.

Tariq unwrapped the scarf from his face and drank his juice in two long gulps, then licked his lips and nodded to the fat woman behind the counter, asking for a refill.

Ben, Frank and Kitkat had a hundred questions for Tariq, but they began by asking what he had been doing in the Jemma al Fna last night.

"Why were you fighting those two men?" asked Ben. "Who were they?"

"Bad people," said Tariq.

"We could see that," said Kitkat.

"But why were you fighting?" insisted Ben. "What did they do to you? Or what did you do to them?"

"It is complicated," said Tariq. "It is because of *une âne*."

"*Âne*? What's an *âne*?"

"*Une âne*, you know." Tariq put his hands on his head, miming long ears.

"A rabbit?" suggested Kitkat. "They stole your rabbit?"

"No, no. Not rabbit." Leaving his hands on the top of his head, Tariq opened his mouth and made a strange, loud noise, neither a roar nor a neigh, but somewhere in between.

"A horse?" guessed Frank.

"No horse, no. *Une âne*." Tariq waggled his hands on the top of his head and made the same noise again.

"A donkey," said Ben.

Tariq nodded and grinned. "Yes, a donkey. *Une âne* is a donkey."

"I don't understand," said Kitkat. "What's the connection between you and those two men and a donkey?"

"I will tell you," said Tariq.

24

Their conversation was slow and difficult. Tariq took an hour to tell a story that could have been told in ten minutes if the four of them could communicate in the same language. Tariq spoke three fluently – Berber, Arabic and French – but his English was halting and awkward. He spoke in short, curt sentences and paused often to search for words, offering French and Arabic alternatives, then resorting to sign language and mimes.

If Harmony had been there, she could have talked to Tariq in French, but Ben, Frank and Kitkat could only shout out suggestions in English, trying to guess what his mimes meant.

This is what he told them.

He had been born in a small village about a hundred kilometres from Marrakech. He was the oldest child in his family. He had two brothers and four sisters. The youngest was still a little baby.

The family owned a small plot of land, which gave them enough space to grow food for themselves and a little extra to sell. Once a week, Tariq's father loaded baskets with produce, strapped them to their donkey and led it to the market in the nearest town.

A couple of years ago, Tariq's father was returning from the market when he was ambushed by a gang of thieves. He fought as hard as he could, but one man can't overcome six.

They beat him unconscious.

When he came to, he was alone. The gang had gone, taking the cash from his pocket and the donkey too. He picked himself up and stumbled home, arriving in the middle of the night, his face coated with dried blood.

He collapsed on his bed and couldn't get up. Every breath was an effort. If he had been richer, he would have summoned a doctor, but he was just a poor farmer from a tiny village. Doctors didn't bother leaving the towns for men like him.

Each day, the family had less food.

They had no savings. No money. Nothing to live on.

Their neighbours donated whatever they could afford, but no one in the village had much to spare.

One morning, Tariq's mother took him aside and told him what he had to do. He was the oldest, she said. He could look after himself better than the others. He should leave the village and go to Marrakech. There, he would be able to earn enough money to pay his father's medical bills.

Tariq protested, asking how he was supposed to find a job in a strange city where he knew no one, but his mother stroked his cheek and told him that he would be fine. He was clever and resourceful. He would be able to look after himself.

The following morning, Tariq said goodbye to his brothers, his sisters, his mother and his father, and left the village.

He walked for the whole day and slept that night in a field. The next morning, he hitched a lift in a truck which was heading north.

He had never left his village before and arriving at Marrakech was like walking into a dream. There was a single TV in the village, so he'd seen films of cities, but nothing could have prepared him for the colourful, chaotic reality. He was bewildered by the noise, the chaos and, more than anything, the sheer number of people, shouting, talking, pushing through the streets. No one was interested in a homeless, helpless boy from the countryside. No one even spoke to him – apart from the drivers who shouted at him to get out of the way. Why was he blocking the road? Couldn't he see that they needed to get past?

He wandered into the big square at the heart of the city, sat on the ground and wondered what to do.

Around him, people were buying and selling, eating and drinking, laughing and talking. He could see a dancer spinning cartwheels and an old woman offering to tattoo a girl's arm with henna.

Several kids, younger than him, pushed through the crowd, pestering tourists, asking for money or offering their services as a guide. Most of them were sent away with nothing, but one got a gift of several battered coins.

Tariq followed them through the square, watching what they did. Then he did it too.

By nightfall, he'd earned enough to buy a plate of hot, spicy sausages. He slept in the street and started working again in the morning, chasing tourists and asking for some spare change.

Day after day, he wandered around the city, getting to know his way around the maze of streets. He slept where he could, curling up in a dark doorway or the cellar of an abandoned house.

He quickly learnt that tourists were an easy way to make a little money. He had only been in the city for a few days, but he knew enough to work as a guide. If he got lost, he asked directions from a local, speaking in Arabic, and the tourists didn't know what he was doing.

Other children lived like him. Adults too. The Jemma al Fna and the souk were packed with beggars, dancers, actors, acrobats, singers, salesmen and guides, trying to skim a living from the endless crowd of tourists and visitors.

One of the other children introduced him to an old man named Hassan and his two sons, Yusuf and Elias. They owned a shop in the souk, a cave packed with antique carpets and ornamental swords and bejewelled daggers and silver goblets and huge brass bowls and every imaginable wonder that a foreigner might want to buy as a souvenir to take home to his own country.

"You bring tourists to me," Hassan explained. "They will buy souvenirs from my shop. They like to have a bowl or a picture to take home to their own country. I will pay you a twentieth of whatever they spend. Do you understand what that means? Let me explain. If a tourist buys a pair of slippers for a hundred dirhams, I will pay you five. If they buy a carpet for twenty thousand dirhams, I will pay you a thousand. Find a few rich tourists who want to buy nice carpets and you will soon have a shop of your own. Go into the streets, boy. Search for foreigners. Find the foolish ones, the proud ones, the rich ones, and bring them to me."

Some days were good. Tariq would find sleek, well-dressed tourists who carried their cash in thick leather wallets and left the shop laden with souvenirs. They would pay thousands of dirhams for a bronze plate or an ornamental sword, believing that they had acquired a valuable antique. Of course, they didn't know that you could buy the same plate or sword for only fifty dirhams if you went directly to the factory.

Hassan kept his promise, handing over a twentieth of the sum that the tourists had spent. Tariq also earned a little extra from the tourists themselves, who usually tipped their guide with a few dirhams, thanking him for being so polite and helpful.

Last night, Tariq met a group of tourists. A family. They were lost. They wanted to get back to the Riad Gazelle. When he delivered them to their destination, they gave him a big tip. Much more than he was used to. A hundred dirhams.

He bought himself some supper of a boiled egg and a hunk of bread, then headed for the shop.

Yusuf and Elias were lounging on cushions, while Hassan was sitting at the desk, counting money. When he saw Tariq, he tucked the cash into a wooden box and closed the lid. "What do you want? Why are you here now? You should be working."

"I want to make a deal with you," said Tariq.

"Oh, yes? You've become a merchant, have you?"

"I have."

"Very good. I like to see such enterprise in one so young. And what is this deal?"

"I have something that you might want to buy."

"That sounds interesting. What are you selling?"

"This." Tariq reached into his pocket and took out a silver ring studded with three glistening jewels. He placed the ring in the palm of his hand and offered it to Hassan. "Do you want to buy some diamonds?"

25

That was when Ben, Frank and Kitkat interrupted him, all three of them talking at once, demanding an explanation. What was he saying? Where did he get those diamonds? He wasn't the thief, was he?

When they quietened down enough to let him speak, Tariq sadly shrugged his shoulders and admitted everything. "Me, I am the one who done it. Yes, you heard me true. I am the thief. And also I must say this. I am very, very sorry. I make a big mistake."

Ben couldn't believe what he was hearing. He assumed Tariq must be joking or lying. It was the only explanation. He remembered exactly what had happened last night and he knew that there simply hadn't been an opportunity for Tariq to take the ring. He said, "You can't just pull a ring from a woman's finger."

"I can," said Tariq.

"But how? Why didn't she notice what you were doing?"

"*Je suis un bon voleur*. I am a very good thief." Tariq wasn't boasting. Nor was he proud. He was simply stating a fact. "I have many friends who is thief. They tell me tricks. I can take the ring from the finger of the woman, no problem."

"I don't understand," said Kitkat. "Are you a guide or a thief?"

"I am the two," said Tariq. "I can guide good, but also I can steal good. What you want, I can steal it. The wallet, the purse, the watch, the ring, I will take it."

Ben shook his head. "That's just not possible. I was there. I saw what happened. You might be the best thief in the world, but you still couldn't have taken that ring from her finger."

"I will show you." Tariq stood up. "Come, stand."

Ben did as he was told. They stood opposite one another like two cowboys preparing for a duel. Frank, Kitkat and the fat woman watched them intently, waiting to see what would happen.

Tariq raised his right hand and called out to Ben as if he hadn't seen him for months. "*Salut,* Monsieur Ben! How are you, my good friend?"

"I'm fine, thanks," said Ben, playing along. "How are you?"

"I am very happy, because I am seeing you!" Tariq hurried forward and enthusiastically shook Ben's hand with both of his. "Are you well, Monsieur Ben? Are you happy?"

"Very happy, thank you."

"You are happy, I am happy." Tariq chuckled, then threw his arms around Ben and wrapped him in a big bear hug.

Kitkat giggled and Frank watched intently, determined not to miss a thing.

Tariq squeezed Ben tightly and patted him several times on the back. Then he released him, twirled round and grinned to the others as if he'd just performed a magnificent feat. "You see? Congratulations, please! I am good thief, no?"

No one answered. They didn't understand what he was talking about.

"You can't be a very good thief," said Ben. "You didn't actually take anything."

"I think you are wrong, Monsieur Ben." Tariq reached into his pocket and pulled out a slim black object. "You want one phone?" He tossed it across the room.

Ben caught the phone. He recognized it

immediately. "You stole my phone! How did you do that?"

"Like I tell you. I am good thief."

The others gave him a round of applause – Frank, Kitkat and the fat woman too – and crowded round, demanding to know how he had done it, but Tariq refused to give away any of his secrets.

Ben stared at his phone. He didn't want to applaud. He wasn't impressed by what Tariq had done. No, he was surprised and disappointed. And, worst of all, he felt like a complete idiot. He had been wrong about everything.

He'd drawn up a ludicrous list of suspects – all of whom were innocent. He'd created a cunning plan which involved his sister breaking the law and putting herself in prison.

And for what? To save a thief!

But it wasn't entirely his fault. He had been cheated and duped. Tariq had made him look like an idiot.

So what were they going to do now?

First things first. They should get Harmony out of prison. She shouldn't be locked behind bars while the real thief was free to walk away.

He said, "You know what, Tariq? If you're such a

good thief, we should take you back to prison. That's where you belong."

Tariq looked panicked. "No, please. Not prison. I will do anything, but no police, no prison."

"Don't worry," said Kitkat. "He's only joking."

"Not very funny," said Tariq.

Ben said, "Actually, I'm not joking. Our sister is in prison. We left her there in exchange for you. She's taking a huge risk on your behalf. If you're the thief and you stole the ring, why did we get you out of there?"

"Because you are good people."

"Yes, but you're not."

"You are true. I am a bad person." Tariq tried to look contrite, but his cheeky grin gave away his true feelings. He couldn't help chuckling at his own good fortune; he had stolen a ring and then been released from prison by the very people that he had stolen it from. "Look, my friend, I will tell you this. Sometimes it is good to be a bad person. For instance, we will find your diamonds, yes? This is why you have need of me."

"So where is it?" said Kitkat. "Where's the ring?"

26

Tariq wouldn't let go of the ring, so Hassan came round the desk and peered down at the three diamonds, staring at them for a long time. Then he lifted his head and stared into the boy's eyes.

"Yes, I will take them. Name your price."

Tariq didn't know how to answer. He was sure that the ring was valuable, but he had no idea what it might actually be worth. In the past, if he stole a watch or a bracelet, he simply brought it to Hassan, who always paid a decent amount, peeling notes from the bundle in the wooden box.

But this was different. This was his best haul yet. If he was careful and cunning, the ring should earn him enough to leave Marrakech for ever. He could pay his father's medical bills and buy a donkey to replace the one that had been stolen.

He knew he had to say something, so he

plucked a figure out of the air. "A hundred thousand dirhams."

Hassan snorted derisively. "You're joking, aren't you? Those aren't even diamonds. They're just toys. I'll give you a hundred dirhams."

"You're lying," said Tariq. "They're real diamonds."

"How do you know? Are you an expert? Can you recognize a diamond when you see one?"

Tariq closed his hand around the ring. "If you don't want them, I'll take them to another shop."

"You don't have to do that," said Hassan. "You're a good boy and you've brought me a lot of good business. I'd like to reward you for all your hard work. To say thank you, I'll take that old ring from you – and I'll give you a thousand dirhams."

"I already told you my price," said Tariq. "I won't take a thousand. I want a hundred thousand."

Hassan chuckled. "You drive a hard bargain. You must have been learning from me! You're a good student and I like you, so how about this. I'll give you two thousand dirhams."

"No."

"You won't take two thousand dirhams?"

"It's not enough." Tariq tried to keep his

expression calm, showing none of the nervousness that he actually felt. Two thousand dirhams was a vast sum, but he was sure he could get much more. If Hassan was willing to offer so much so quickly, then the diamonds must be worth a vast amount. "You can have it for ninety thousand dirhams."

"You know that's impossible," said Hassan. "I can't offer you any more than two thousand. That's my final offer. Two thousand dirhams. If you have any sense, you'll take it."

"Eighty thousand."

"Two thousand five hundred."

"Seventy-five thousand."

"Three thousand. And that's my final offer."

"Seventy thousand," said Tariq. "Or nothing."

"Then it will have to be nothing." Hassan nodded to his two sons.

Yusuf and Elias eased themselves to their feet, surrounding Tariq and blocking his escape route. They raised their arms, curling their fingers into fists.

Tariq knew there was no point trying to fight. Three of them against one of him – three adults against one boy – he didn't have a hope. He tried to protest, but they advanced on him and he saw that he faced a simple choice: give up his prize or get hurt. He tried to say that he'd changed his mind and would take three thousand dirhams, but it was too late. He'd missed his chance. Hassan was now determined to get the three diamonds for nothing.

Cursing his own stupidity, Tariq handed over the ring.

It was his own fault. He knew that Hassan, Yusuf and Elias were thieves. He had seen how they cheated foreigners. Why did he imagine that they would treat him any differently?

Yusuf delivered the ring to his father, who opened a drawer in a tall cabinet at the back of the shop and lifted out a little magnifying glass.

Hassan pored over the diamonds, peering at them through the glass, then straightened up and congratulated Tariq on his skills. "You have done well, my child. These are very valuable. You could have sold these and bought a hundred donkeys for your father. No – a thousand. If you had offered me a good deal, I would have rewarded you with more riches than you can imagine. You could have gone home and showered your village with money. But I shall give you nothing. Now, go away. Go back to the streets where you belong." He flicked his wrist at Tariq, dismissing him, then returned to studying the diamonds. Yusuf and Elias settled back on their cushions, sipping mint tea and smiling at their father's cunning.

Tariq knew what he was supposed to do. Turn round, walk out of the shop, go back to the streets and search for tourists. But a sudden fury drove him forward. He lunged for the wooden box, snatched it from the desk and sprinted out of the doorway. He heard shouts behind him, but he didn't pause or look back.

As he ran through the souk, he realized what he had done.

He had seen how the old man dealt with anyone who wronged him. A saddle-maker had failed to pay a debt of four thousand dirhams. Yusuf and Elias snapped the four fingers on his left hand. A drunk barged into Hassan in the street and didn't apologize. Yusuf and Elias chased after him, tripped him over and beat him senseless.

What would they do to a boy who stole their money?

If they didn't kill him, they would certainly break most of his bones.

What should he do? Where could he hide?

Not in the city. Hassan knew everyone in Marrakech and someone would be sure to tell him where Tariq was hiding. No, he had to go further.

To Casablanca. The biggest city in Morocco. They would never find him there. With the money in the box, he might even be able to smuggle himself into Spain or France and start a new life in Madrid or Paris. He'd work hard and earn money. Ten years from now, he would return to Marrakech, dressed in a silk suit, and stroll into Hassan's shop. They would think that he was just another wealthy tourist wanting to spend a few hundred dollars.

Yes, he thought. That's perfect. That's what I want to do. Get out of Morocco. Go to Europe. Make money. Turn myself into a rich man.

First things first. He had to get out of Marrakech as fast as possible.

He would go to the bus station and catch the first bus heading north. And then he would be free.

He emerged on one side of the Jemma al Fna and sprinted across the square, heading for the main road that led to the bus station.

He heard a shout.

Yusuf and Elias were running towards him. They must have guessed that he would come this way.

He whirled round and sprinted in the opposite direction.

The two brothers powered after him, pushing people aside, ignoring their cries and complaints.

Tariq tried to conceal himself among the dancers and the musicians, the boxers and the snake charmers, but he wasn't quick enough. Yusuf grabbed his sleeve. Tariq jumped backwards, but Elias was ready for him. He was trapped between them.

People stepped backwards, clearing a space, giving them room.

Yusuf and Elias advanced on him slowly.

Tariq had nowhere to go, nowhere to hide. He threw the cashbox at the brothers, hoping that they would lose interest in him when they got their money back, but it didn't work. They wanted to punish him for his insolence.

A crowd gathered. The Jemma al Fna is always packed with performers and people must have thought that this was just another show.

Tariq thought someone would help him, but the crowd of tourists and locals just stood and watched, applauding every kick and punch. He begged for help, crying out that he was going to be killed, but his words were greeted by laughter. He knew why. They thought he was an actor and his screams were part of the show.

He knew what would happen next. Yusuf and Elias would knock him to the ground and break his bones. The crowd would carry on cheering till his ribs had been snapped and blood was pouring out of his ears.

Then a foreign boy stepped out of the crowd with both hands raised and said in a loud, clear voice: "Stop!"

27

The black cat slept through Tariq's performance, but the fat woman leaned on the counter and watched him intently, tearing herself away with unconcealed reluctance on the rare occasions that another customer came into the café and ordered a cup of coffee. She spoke a little French and no English, so she could hardly follow what he was saying, but she enjoyed the moments when he sprang from the table and stood in the middle of the room, acting out a scene from his life. Now he had finished, she emerged from behind the counter and refilled their glasses from a jug of orange juice, waving away Frank's offer of payment.

"I've never heard such a horrible story," said Kitkat. "It's so unfair. How can people be like that? What's wrong with them?" She turned to her brothers. "We have to help him."

"What are you talking about?" asked Ben. "He stole the diamonds, remember? He's the bad guy."

"No, he's not. Hassan is. And Yusuf and Elias too. They took his ring."

"It's not his ring," said Ben. "It's Celia's."

"That's true, but. . ." Kitkat rubbed her head, thinking through the muddled morality of the various thefts. Finally she sighed and shook her head. "Oh, I don't know. It's all so complicated. They're all bad in their own ways. But I still think we should help Tariq. He only stole the ring because he wanted to buy a donkey for his dad. That's sweet, isn't it?"

"I don't know if 'sweet' is quite the right word."

"He is sweet," said Kitkat confidently. She had been won over by Tariq's charm. Looking at his frizzy hair, his goofy smile and his skinny limbs poking out of Harmony's skirt and blouse, she felt affectionate and very protective. He might have done some bad things in his life, but she was convinced that he wasn't a bad person. "The Misfitz are going to help him. And in return, he's going to help us. He'll take us to Hassan. We'll get the diamonds and give them back to Celia. The police will put Hassan, Yusuf and Elias in prison, so they won't want to torture Tariq. And everyone will be happy. You'll do that for us, won't you?"

"I will do anything for you," said Tariq.

"Perfect." Kitkat rubbed her hands together, ready for the next stage of their adventure. "Let's go and find those diamonds."

"There's only one problem," said Ben. "Where are they?"

Tariq told them what he knew.

If you walked past Hassan's shop, you would see carpets, lamps, plates and bowls hanging in the windows. If you went inside, you would find even more. But these weren't his most valuable goods.

If a rich tourist came to the shop, Hassan would send one of his sons down to the cellar to fetch a gold plate or a sword in a scabbard encrusted with sapphires.

There was only one entrance to the cellar: a wooden hatch in the floor at the back of the shop. Tariq had never been allowed into the cellar himself, and never dared to sneak down there, but he knew that the most valuable items – such as a diamond ring – were kept in a metal safe secured with a large padlock. Hassan kept the key in his desk.

"Let me get this straight," said Frank. "We just

have to go to the shop, get past Hassan and his sons, steal the key, open the hatch, walk down the steps to the cellar, unlock the safe, find the diamonds and then get out again."

"Correct," said Tariq.

"How are we supposed to do that?"

Tariq gave a hopeless shrug of his shoulders as if to say: *that's your problem*.

"How about the police?" suggested Kitkat. "Couldn't they help us?"

"*Non, non*," said Tariq, waving his hands in the air. "No police."

"He's been to the police already," said Ben. "You saw what they did to him."

"They might change their mind if we were there too."

"They won't," said Frank. "We've broken the law, remember? We took him out of prison. They'll chuck Tariq in a cell and us with him."

Kitkat frowned. "Benjy, what about your dad? Couldn't he help us?"

"No way," said Ben. "You know what he's like. You can't trust him to do anything."

"Then what are we going to do?"

"We have to come up with a brilliant plan."

"Like what?"

"I don't know."

Kitkat turned to her other brother. "You're clever, Frankie. Can't you think of a brilliant plan?"

Frank shook his head. "To be honest, it's not looking good. We'd have to break into a shop and overcome three men. Possibly armed. Certainly dangerous. Even worse, we'll be attacking them on their own territory. Even if we managed to outwit them, we'd have to go down into a cellar, find the ring and get out again. How are we supposed to do that? We're not exactly the SAS, are we? We're just three kids in a foreign country where we don't know anyone or anything."

Kitkat said, "As soon as we get Harmony out of prison, there'll be four of us."

"Five if you count Tariq," said Ben.

"Five kids," said Frank. "What can we do against a gang of ruthless Moroccan thieves?"

We can't give up, thought Ben. But what else can we do?

Who could they turn to for help?

No one.

They had to do it themselves.

But how?

Whatever they did, they had to work fast. They

didn't have much time. Ben was sure of that. Hassan would soon find a buyer for such valuable booty.

He probably wouldn't try to sell the ring as it was. Instead, he'd break the jewels from their setting and sell them to a diamond dealer.

They wouldn't even stay in Marrakech. Tomorrow or next week, if you went into a jewellery shop in Casablanca, you might see a beautiful gold necklace strung with a single glittering diamond. You'd never guess it had once been attached to a silver ring.

They had to stop that happening.

But how?

No one else seemed to have any ideas. Frank was slumped in one chair and Tariq in another, staring at the ceiling.

The black cat uncurled itself, paced across the floor and sprang into Kitkat's lap. She stroked its ears and the cat purred loudly.

Maybe we should forget the diamonds, thought Ben. Harmony is still in prison. She's been there for hours now. She must be lonely, uncomfortable and thoroughly miserable. Shouldn't we get her out again?

If she was here, what would she say?

Would she want them to forget the diamonds and rescue her instead?

No, of course she wouldn't.

"Don't worry about me," she'd say. "I'm perfectly capable of looking after myself. Just find those diamonds."

And she would be right.

The only question was: how?

Maybe Frank was right. They were just a bunch of kids in a foreign country. They couldn't speak the language and they couldn't find their way around. How were they supposed to stop a gang of thieves?

We can't give up, thought Ben. We have to do something.

But what?

He remembered that he had been in similar situations before. Everything had seemed hopeless. He had been confronted by impossible problems and insoluble mysteries. But he'd managed to find a way out. There was always something that could be done.

You just have to create a plan.

A brilliant plan.

But what?

He thought about the shop and the safe and the

cellar. He thought about Hassan and Yusuf and Elias. He thought about himself and Frank and Kitkat and Tariq. He thought about Harmony, locked in her cell, and the three diamonds, down in a cellar.

And then he had an idea.

28

The taxi dropped Robert and Celia at the edge of the souk. By now, Robert had walked the streets enough times that he really could find his own way to the Riad Gazelle.

The door was opened by Mohammed, who greeted them with a wide smile. "*Ah, Monsieur! Madame! Vous êtes retournez!* You did see the lawyer? He was good?"

"He seemed very sensible," said Robert. "He's going to meet us at the police station and help us cut through some of the crazy bureaucracy. I wanted to come back here first and see the kids. Have they given you any trouble?"

"*Non, non*, they are perfect," said Mohammed. "I hear nothing. No noise. No problem. They are very good."

Robert could only claim any credit for two of the children, but he still felt oddly proud that they had all behaved so well. He asked Mohammed to bring some mint tea and a few croissants to the roof terrace, then went upstairs to congratulate the kids on their behaviour.

When he arrived on the roof terrace, he found their books and magazines, but no sign of the children themselves. Maybe they were catching up on lost sleep. He went downstairs to wake them up.

All three bedrooms were empty.

Mohammed promised that they couldn't have left the riad. He had been stationed by the door all morning and there wasn't another exit.

"They might be playing a game," suggested Celia. "When I was a kid, I loved hide-and-seek. Maybe they heard us coming back and decided to hide."

Robert, Celia and Mohammed searched every corner of the riad, checking every room, opening the cupboards and peering under the beds, but they couldn't find any sign of Frank, Harmony, Kitkat or Ben.

They trudged up to the roof terrace and sorted through the books and magazines scattered across the table, searching for a clue.

Celia was the first to notice the ladder.

"This is impossible," said Mohammed, looking

at the wobbly ladder and the long drop down to the street. "No one is doing this."

"Sadly, that's not true." Robert had heard enough stories from his ex-wife to know what his children were capable of.

They raced downstairs, hurried along the street, knocked on the door of the neighbouring riad and quizzed the housemaid. She confirmed what they had already guessed.

Robert rang Ben, Frank and Harmony. (Kitkat was too young to have a phone of her own.) He left angry messages on their answerphones, demanding to know where they were and what they were doing.

"You could ring your ex-wife," said Celia. "She might have a useful suggestion."

Robert shook his head. "No way. I'm not getting her involved. She'll just say 'I told you so.'"

"We could go to the police."

"I want them to concentrate on finding your diamonds. Don't worry, honey, I know where the kids will be. They're on holiday in a foreign country and they just want to have fun. They've sneaked out to see the snake charmers. Let's go to the big square and find them."

*

Ben and Frank had turned their phones to silent, but they saw that Robert had rung them: Ben first, then Frank.

Ben considered ringing his dad back and inventing some story, but decided not to bother. Over the past few years, his father had kept him waiting often enough. For once, it was Robert's turn to wait.

Anyway, Ben was too busy to make any phone calls.

He was sitting at the table with the others. Three sheets of paper were spread before them.

On the first sheet, Tariq had drawn a map of the streets surrounding Hassan's shop.

A cross marked the shop itself.

A dotted line showed Tariq's route.

Two smaller crosses showed where Frank would be waiting and where he would move to.

Tariq had drawn a quick sketch of the shop on the second sheet of paper, showing the positions of the entrance, Hassan's desk, the door into the kitchen, the carpet and the hatch that led to the cellar. He had indicated where Kitkat should go with Hassan so Ben couldn't be seen.

The third sheet was divided into four columns, one for each of them, showing what they had to do and when.

They could have added a fifth column for Harmony, but there didn't seem much point. She would simply be sitting in her cell, waiting for them to come and collect her. It was frustrating. Her presence would have been extremely useful. But they couldn't think of any way to get her out of prison.

Ben checked with the others, asking if they had memorized the map, the sketch and the schedule.

Everyone had.

Ben folded up the three sheets and tucked them in his pocket. "Let's go and rob a thief."

29

Harmony could hear footsteps in the corridor. She tugged the hoodie over her face and turned to face the wall.

The footsteps stopped at the next cell. She heard voices and a rattling noise. Someone was visiting her neighbour.

She sat back and relaxed, not sure whether to be relieved or disappointed.

She wouldn't have admitted it to anyone, but she couldn't help hoping that the footsteps belonged to Inspector Mahmoud, coming to interrogate Tariq. He would pull the hoodie from her face and discover the true identity of his prisoner. He'd probably be furious – no, he'd definitely be furious – but at least she wouldn't have to spend any more time alone in this cell.

She wanted to get out of here.

Her legs ached. Her arms too. She was tired and

lonely and cold and uncomfortable and very, very bored.

She had always imagined that prison would be quite fun. She liked her own company and she was usually perfectly content to be left alone. She didn't mind sitting on a train, for instance, staring out of the window for hours and daydreaming about her life, her friends, her family and the future.

There was no logical reason that prison should have been any different. A silent cell should have been a good place to do some serious thinking. But not a single interesting thought had entered her mind, which remained resolutely fixed on the discomforts of the here and now. She felt awkward and ashamed. She was desperate to pee, but she didn't dare squat on the bucket in case the guard unexpectedly opened the peephole. Worst of all, the simple fact of being unable to leave this room filled her with a frantic urge to get out.

She heard more footsteps in the corridor. This time, they stopped outside her cell.

She curled against the wall, hiding her face.

Keys rattled. The lock clicked. The door swung open. A policeman took two quick steps into the cell and placed a tray on the floor. He hardly glanced at the figure on the bed, just grunted a couple of words in Arabic, then went out again.

Harmony waited till the policeman had locked her door and gone further down the corridor, then perched on the edge of the bed and peered at her lunch.

This is what she had been given:

A bowl of brown soup dotted with a few soggy chunks which might have been potato.

A slice of a hard white bread.

A cup of warm water.

Harmony knew she shouldn't drink the water, but she had no choice. She didn't want to die of thirst. The soup was tasteless, but she ate it anyway, mopping up the last scraps with the stale bread. Then she lay on the bench, tugged the hoodie over her face and closed her eyes. Time would pass faster if she fell asleep.

30

From Tariq's description, Ben had formed a solid mental image of Hassan, his sons and his shop, but he was surprised to discover that the reality was very different. For one thing, the shop was much bigger than he had imagined. When he and Kitkat stepped through the entrance, they found themselves in what appeared to be a long, thin, darkly lit warehouse cluttered with treasures of all shapes and sizes. An endless variety of carpets hung from the walls. Ornate lanterns and candelabra dangled from the low ceiling. Hundreds of plates and bowls, decorated in every imaginable colour and design, were stacked in wooden shelves. The rest of the shop was crammed with statues, books, clothes, silver swords, rusty tools, old clocks, leather saddles and an endless variety of mysterious objects that Ben couldn't begin to identify.

You could spend a week searching this shop, thought Ben. And you'd never find a ring.

Two men were lounging on cushions. Both looked about twenty. They were clean-shaven. One was wearing jeans and an Arsenal T-shirt. That must be Elias. The other was dressed more traditionally in leather sandals and a long white robe. He was Yusuf.

A third man was sitting behind a large wooden desk. Ben had imagined a wrinkled old man with a long white beard, but Hassan looked vigorous and energetic. He couldn't have been much more than forty. He had piercing dark eyes and a neatly trimmed black beard, streaked with a few grey hairs. He glanced at the two foreign children who had wandered into his shop, wondering what they wanted. *"Oui? Bonjour? Puis-je vous aider?"*

"Do you speak English?" Ben asked hesitantly. He already knew the answer to his question, of course. Tariq had briefed them about Hassan, Yusuf, Elias and the geography of the shop. But he needed to pretend that he knew nothing about them.

"Yes, I can speak a little English," replied Hassan. "How can I help you? You are lost? You are looking for your hotel?"

"We want to buy a present for our mother."

"Please, look around." Hassan gestured at the depths of his shop. "You will find something."

"Thank you." Ben smiled shyly. As if it was an afterthought, he said, "We only have six hundred dollars. Do you think that might be enough to buy a nice present?"

Hassan stroked his beard and tried to pretend that he wasn't interested. "And for this money, what do you hope for?"

"A carpet," said Ben.

"Just a small one," explained Kitkat. "It has to fit in our luggage."

"It doesn't have to be anything fancy," added Ben. "It's our mum's birthday, you see. Our dad gave us some money and told us to buy her a present. We saw the carpets hanging outside your shop. She'd love one of them."

Hassan grinned. He could see that he was going to earn some easy money today. He stepped round the desk and came to greet them personally. "I will be happy to help, my young friends. I will find you a very good carpet. You have come to the right place. My name is Hassan and I have the best carpets in Marrakech." He pulled two small chairs from the wall. "Please, sit down. Will you take some tea?"

"Tea would be lovely," said Kitkat.

Hassan snapped his fingers at his sons and issued an order in Arabic. Yusuf lazily hauled himself to his feet and went through a curtain into a dark room behind Hassan's desk. Elias wandered into the back of the shop. When he returned, his arms were weighed down with a stack of tightly scrolled carpets. He lowered them to the floor.

"We will show you some carpets," said Hassan. "No buying, just looking. You must say what you like. No need to worry, we will find the perfect present for your mother." He nodded to Elias, who unscrolled a carpet with a deft flick of his wrists and laid it on the floor.

"Oh, it's beautiful," said Kitkat.

Ben said, "How much is it?"

Hassan smiled. "Please, like I say, no buying. Just looking." He nodded to Elias, who unrolled another carpet on top of the first, then another. Each carpet was woven in glorious colours, reds and golds, blues and browns. You could have sat and stared at them for hours, letting your eyes wander around the swirls and along the borders, following the harmonious lines of the symmetrical patterns.

Hassan gave a running commentary, explaining

that one carpet came from a tiny village on the opposite side of the Atlas Mountains and owed its amazing colours to a particular flower that could only be found on those hillsides. Another had been woven by Bedouin women and crossed the desert on the back of a camel. A third had spent the last century hanging on a bedroom wall in one of the king's many palaces.

Yusuf pushed through the curtain carrying a silver tray laden with a teapot, a sugar bowl and five small glasses. He placed the tray on a low table and was just about to pour the tea when he noticed a small figure standing in the doorway, silhouetted by the sharp sunlight. Yusuf straightened up and spoke to his father in a low voice.

That was when Tariq started shouting.

He was speaking Arabic, so Ben couldn't understand a word, but he knew what Tariq had been planning to say. He was going to shower Hassan with insults, calling him a thief, a liar, an idiot, a cheat, a goat, a pig and the son of a camel.

Hassan listened for a moment, then yelled at his sons. His face was red and his eyes flashed with fury.

Go on, thought Ben. Let the blood rush to your head.

When you're angry, you can't think clearly. You

make mistakes. You can be fooled more easily.

Following their father's orders, Yusuf and Elias hurled themselves at the figure in the doorway.

Tariq had been expecting them to do exactly that. He darted out of the shop, tossing a few final curses over his shoulder.

Yusuf and Elias were only a few paces behind him. They were much bigger than the skinny little kid. Stronger too. And their legs were longer. They wouldn't have any trouble catching him.

When his sons had gone, Hassan composed himself quickly and turned his attention back to his customers. "I am most sorry," he said with a calm smile. "This is a bad boy."

"Do you know him?" asked Ben.

"Oh, yes. I know him very good."

"Who is he?"

"Just a boy," said Hassan. "He steals from me."

Kitkat gasped. Her hand flew to her mouth. "How terrible! What did he steal?"

"Oh, it is nothing important. Forget about him. Let us talk about carpets. Tell me, please, what is the favourite colour of your mother?"

31

Frank was ready. He was standing by a stall in a narrow, shadowy alleyway, pretending to examine a display of brightly painted cups, bowls, plates, jugs and ashtrays, but all his attention was actually focused on the entrance to Hassan's shop. A moment ago, he had seen Tariq walk through the doorway. Now he was waiting for him to come out again.

And here he was, running down the alley at full speed. Tariq was still wearing Harmony's clothes, but they didn't slow him down. He'd tucked the skirt into its own waistband, keeping it out of his way. He dodged past a pedestrian and ducked under a shopkeeper's outstretched arm, heading straight for Frank.

A man came after him.

And then another.

Anyone in their way got knocked aside.

Frank waited for the perfect moment and then extended his right leg. He'd been worried that he would mess it up, but he managed to time his move impeccably, avoiding Tariq and the first of the men, then hooking his foot around the second man's ankle.

Yusuf went flying.

He somersaulted through the air, skidded across a puddle and sprawled into the middle of the crockery stall. His head smashed through a fruit bowl. His shoulders thumped into a display of cups and ashtrays. A row of plates cascaded on to the pavement and broke in a hundred pieces.

Alerted by the noise, Elias whirled round and looked back to see what had happened. Should he double back and help his brother? Or catch the boy? What would his father want him to do? The answer was obvious. He sprinted after the fleeing figure of Tariq.

Yusuf sat up, clutching his head.

The shopkeeper yelled at him, demanding to know who was going to pay for all these broken plates.

Yusuf took no notice. He pulled himself to his feet, shaking shards of crockery from his clothes, and looked around, searching for the idiot who had tripped him up. He'd caught a quick glimpse of a skinny foreign boy with black-rimmed glasses and a black T-shirt.

Whoever he was, he'd gone.

He didn't have time to search for him now. There was a thief to be caught. Yusuf shoved the shopkeeper aside, ignoring his protests, and ran after his brother.

Frank stepped out of the shadows.

The first part of the plan had worked perfectly. He just hoped the second part would go equally well.

He ducked under an archway, hurried through a deserted courtyard and soon arrived in another alleyway much like the first, packed with shops and stalls. He selected a good hiding place, positioning himself between a stall selling spices and a butcher's shop barricaded with live chickens in wicker cages, squawking furiously as if they had already guessed their own fate.

32

Inside the shop, they heard the sound of smashing crockery. Hassan would have gone outside to investigate, but Kitkat sprang to her feet and intercepted him. "Can I look round the rest of your shop? There's so much lovely stuff here. Maybe we shouldn't get a carpet for our mum. Maybe we should get a bowl or a sword or something else instead."

"Please, be my guest. My shop is your home."

Kitkat browsed the stacked shelves. She picked up an earthenware pot, examined a string of beads and put a brass bugle to her lips. Each treasure led her further and deeper into the shadows at the back of the shop.

Hassan asked Ben to choose his favourite from the carpets that they had seen so far. "Not for buying. Just for conversation. Tell me what you like."

"That one." Ben picked a carpet at random. "But it's too small."

"Then we will find bigger." Hassan hauled several carpets from a shelf behind his desk and spread them on the floor one by one, telling Ben to stop him when he saw one that he liked.

From the distant depths of the shop, Kitkat cried, "Oh! I love this! *Monsieur?* How much is it, *monsieur?*"

Hassan couldn't see what she was talking about. "Excuse me. Do you mind to wait here? I must talk to your sister."

"I don't mind at all," said Ben.

He stayed where he was, squatting on a low chair, a cup of tea in his hand, till Hassan had disappeared behind stacks of antiques. Then he put down his tea and darted across the room, running round to the back of the desk. The carpets muffled his footsteps.

He knew he didn't have much time. Kitkat would ask all kinds of irritating questions – she was good at doing that – but she'd only be able to keep Hassan occupied for a few minutes and then he'd start wondering what had happened to her brother. He wouldn't want to leave a boy alone in the front of the shop. Even a rich tourist with six hundred dollars in his pocket.

Ben opened the top left-hand drawer and pushed his arm through the jumble of papers and envelopes. At the back of the drawer, just as Tariq had promised, his hands closed around a spiky bunch of keys. He took the whole bunch, closed the drawer and stepped through the curtain into the kitchen.

There was a shabby brown carpet on the floor.

Ben kicked it aside to reveal a wooden trapdoor. He hooked his fingers through the handle and pulled it up.

A flight of wooden stairs descended into the gloom.

Ben placed his right foot tentatively on the first step. It wobbled, but didn't give way. Taking the keys and the padlock with him, he padded down the staircase and lowered the trapdoor above his head.

When the door clicked shut, darkness embraced him. He couldn't even see his own hands.

There was a curious mixture of smells – damp and polish and mothballs and spices – jumbled together into one mysterious perfume.

He pulled the lighter from his pocket and flicked the wheel. The flint struck. A little flame shot up.

Now he could see more of his surroundings. The

small, gloomy space felt like a cave cut out of the earth. Crowded shelves ran round the walls, stacked with treasures. And there, squatting on the floor, was a large metal safe, half as tall as Ben himself. The door was secured with a large rusty padlock.

Ben noticed a little stub of a candle, sitting on a shelf in its own white saucer. He lit it.

He knelt on the floor beside the safe and went through the keys, trying them one by one. Finally a slim silver key slotted neatly into the padlock. He unhooked the hasp and swung open the heavy door, then held the candle inside, illuminating the contents, hoping the flame would spark an answering glitter.

33

Robert suggested splitting up so they could cover more ground, but Celia refused. "We've already lost four children," she said. "We don't want to lose one another too."

They wandered round the Jemma al Fna, peering at the market stalls, the white-coated men selling orange juice, the dancers, the beggars, the boxers and the musicians, scouring every face that they saw, but they couldn't find the kids.

Celia suggested calling the police or the embassy, but Robert insisted on making one final circuit of the square. They walked slowly, looking everywhere, watching the endless variety of faces that streamed past.

There was a sudden commotion on the other side of the square. A young girl was weaving through the crowd, trying to escape from two grown men, who were shouting and waving their arms as they pursued her across the Jemma al Fna.

There was something odd about the girl. She was holding her skirt in her hands, pulling it almost to her waist, freeing her legs so she could run more easily.

Celia was amazed. In a country where women modestly cover their faces and their arms, such a brazen display of bare flesh was probably enough to get you arrested.

Then Celia saw the girl's face.

For a moment, she was too surprised to react. She couldn't quite believe what she was seeing. Was that Tariq? But what was he doing here? And why was he dressed in women's clothes? Then she grabbed Robert's arm and told him what she'd just seen.

"That's impossible," said Robert. "You've mixed him up with someone else. There are so many kids here and they all look the same."

Celia pointed across the square. "Look! Some guy's chasing him! He must have stolen something from him too."

Now Robert could see that she was right. There was Tariq, darting through the crowd, pursued by a fit young man in a T-shirt and brand new jeans.

Tariq couldn't have noticed Robert and Celia yet. He was coming straight towards them.

And what was he wearing? That skirt was familiar. Those clothes looked like. . .

No time to worry about that now. Here he came. How were they going to stop him?

Robert and Celia threw out their arms, ready to catch him.

At the last moment, Tariq saw them. He changed course and dodged to the left, pushing past a tourist who was taking a photo of an old woman with no teeth.

Celia yelled: "STOP! THIEF!"

Celia was an actress. Her voice had been trained to fill theatres. When she took a deep breath and shouted with the full force of her powerful lungs, she could be heard for miles. All around the square, people turned and stared, wondering what was happening.

Celia shouted again – "STOP!" – and then gave chase.

Robert ran after her.

Tariq put his head down and sprinted across the Jemma al Fna.

Robert and Celia were pursuing him from one

direction and Elias from another, but Tariq still might have got away if two plain-clothes policemen hadn't been alerted by Celia's screams.

Late last night, these two policemen had been wandering through the crowds when they saw four foreign children chasing a thief across the square. They had caught him and taken him to the police station. He'd been locked up in a secure cell. Now, to their amazement, they saw the same thief, fleeing from another couple of foreigners.

The two policemen stepped out of the crowd with their arms raised and ordered Tariq to stop.

Tariq changed course once more, but he had nowhere to go. One of the policemen grabbed him and twisted both his arms behind his back, then flung him to the ground. The other interrogated Celia and Robert, asking what the boy had done to them.

Elias stepped into the shelter of the crowd and pretended to be listening to a storyteller with a grey beard and a long white robe. He didn't want to get involved with the police. They might ask all sorts of awkward questions. When he saw that they were taking Tariq away, he turned round, pushed through the crowd and went to find his brother.

Back in the souk, Frank was getting impatient.

He glanced at the display on his phone, ignoring the missed calls from Robert and checking the time. He had already been waiting here for five minutes. Tariq was late. Something must have gone wrong.

What should he do? Go back to the shop? Ring Ben? Or wait here in case Tariq had taken a detour?

He rang Ben, but the call went straight to answerphone.

He decided to hold his position for another two minutes. Then he would go and investigate.

34

Kitkat asked all kinds of questions, trying to keep Hassan interested and prevent him returning to the front of the shop. She grabbed a brass plate engraved with long lines of Arabic script and asked for a translation. She found a large leather elephant leaking straw through its seams and demanded to know its name. She saw a clock stamped with the date and place of its manufacture, BLACKBURN 1864, and told Hassan about her friend Meena who had been born in Blackburn but moved to London when she was two years old. "On her fifteenth birthday, she's going to be sent to Bangladesh to get married. Her parents have already chosen her husband, but she hasn't even met him. I keep telling her to run away, but she doesn't want to make her mum upset. What do you think she should do? If you were her, what would you do?"

Hassan was just considering how to answer this

question when his thoughts were interrupted by a sudden commotion at the front of the shop. Yusuf had returned and he was calling to his father.

"Excuse me," said Hassan and went to see what he wanted.

Kitkat followed him nervously, not sure what to do. Why was Yusuf back so quickly? That hadn't been part of the plan.

Hassan noticed that someone was missing. "Where is your brother?"

"Oh." Kitkat looked around innocently. "I don't know. I suppose he must have gone."

"Gone?" Hassan was suspicious. "Why would he go without you?"

"He's always doing things like that. I'll go and look for him."

She marched to the door.

Yusuf was blocking her way.

Kitkat tried to dodge round him, but Yusuf wouldn't let her past.

"Excuse me," said Kitkat. "Could I get out, please?"

Yusuf looked to his father for instructions.

Hassan stared at Kitkat, wondering whether to keep her here and question her further. Then he realized that he was being foolish. She couldn't have been more than seven years old. How could she possibly harm him? He nodded to his son.

Yusuf stepped aside.

"Thank you very much." Kitkat hurried out of the door before Hassan could change his mind.

As soon as she got into the street, Kitkat shielded her eyes against the fierce sunlight and looked for Ben, Frank or Tariq, but she couldn't see any of them. Where could they be? Had Tariq outwitted Yusuf and Elias? Had Frank stopped them catching him? And where was Ben? Had he managed to liberate the ring? Or was he still stuck in the cellar?

She couldn't answer any of these questions, but she knew what to do. At the end of the alleyway, there was a stall selling every imaginable variety of fresh and dried spices. That was where they had arranged to meet if anything went wrong.

Kitkat lingered by the far side of the stall, hidden behind tall glass jars packed with cardamom pods, cumin seeds, cinnamon sticks and fiery scarlet chillies. Cages held worms, beetles, squirrels, sparrows, thrushes, toads and even a scaly-skinned chameleon, his eyes flicking from side to side, nervously scrutinizing passers-by. Perhaps he knew that, just like the other creatures in the shop, he was destined to be sold to a witch or a magician, who would drop him in a cauldron of boiling water and transform him into a love potion, a cure for sleepless nights or an ointment guaranteed to remove warts.

Sheltered by the jars and the cages, Kitkat could see the entrance to Hassan's shop, but she couldn't be seen. She'd wait here. Sooner or later, one of the boys would come back and find her.

35

At the front of the safe, Ben found a heap of banknotes and a neat pile of credit cards. Behind them, stacked against the back wall, there was a plump leather bag, a curved dagger in a scabbard, an ornate silver necklace, six expensive cameras and about twenty phones.

Ben emptied the safe, then ran his hand around the interior, checking for hidden drawers or false walls, but his fingertips encountered nothing except cold metal.

He ruffled through the banknotes.

There were dollars, pounds and euros, and several other currencies that he didn't recognize, printed in scripts that he couldn't read. He didn't bother counting them, but the bundles must have added up to a small fortune.

He tipped out the contents of the leather bag. A delicate gold necklace slithered into his palm, followed by two brooches, three pearl earrings, several wedding rings and a stream of single jewels. Amongst the sapphires, rubies and emeralds, he found a few glittering diamonds, but they looked smaller than the ones that had been fixed to Celia's ring.

He removed the cameras from their cases and pummelled the soft leather, searching for pockets. He switched the cameras on and off again, then opened their battery compartments.

He checked the back and front of every phone.

He inspected every jewel on the necklace.

He pulled the dagger from its scabbard and ran his finger along its polished blade. He rattled the scabbard. There was something inside. He tipped it up and a small silver ring dropped into his palm, glistening with three large diamonds.

Ben grinned. Mission accomplished.

Now he just had to get out of here.

He replaced the contents of the safe, closed the door and secured the padlock. He put the candle where he had found it and blew out the flame. He stood still for a few seconds, waiting for his eyes to adjust to the darkness. Cracks of light defined the floorboards above his head. He climbed the stairs and lifted the trapdoor.

And froze.

He could hear voices. He recognized Hassan's. Was he talking to Kitkat? He heard another voice, also male. That must be Yusuf.

Had the plan failed? Hadn't Frank and Tariq managed to distract both brothers?

No time to worry about that now. Yusuf was here. Hassan too. They would be getting suspicious already, wondering where that foreign boy had gone. Soon they'd come looking for him.

What should he do? Retreat into the cellar and hide? Or get out?

He didn't want to be trapped in the cellar. He scrambled up the last few steps, closed the trapdoor after him and hurriedly shuffled the carpet into position.

He was just about to return to the main shop when he realized that he was still holding the big bunch of keys. Better get rid of them. But where? He looked around, searching for a hiding place, and noticed a teapot. That would do. He lifted the lid and dropped the keys inside. Then he had an idea. He selected a teaspoon from a tray of crockery and stepped through the curtain.

Hassan and Yusuf turned to look at him. There was no sign of Kitkat.

Ben showed them the spoon. "I wanted some sugar in my tea. So I needed one of these."

Hassan pointed at two tiny silver teaspoons lying on the tray beside the teapot and the glasses. "You have already."

"Oh, do I?" Ben pretended to look surprised. "That's funny, I didn't see it."

"Are you stealing my spoon?"

Ben wasn't sure if Hassan was joking or serious, but he laughed anyway. "No, I just needed to stir my tea."

The door swung open and Elias stepped into the shop. He was red-faced and panting. He glanced at Ben, then gabbled a quick explanation to his father and brother.

Hassan issued a curt order.

Elias kicked the door. It swung shut with a bang. The room was dark. Yusuf and Elias stepped forward, taking positions on either side of Ben, blocking any possibility of escape.

Hassan turned to Ben. "You must tell me the truth, please. Why are you here? What you want with me?"

"I've already told you. I want to buy a carpet for my mum."

"Why you go to the kitchen?"

"I needed a spoon. To stir my tea."

"The truth, please. Only the truth. Why are you in the kitchen?"

"I was just looking around," said Ben.

"Looking around? What do you mean?"

"I got bored while you were talking to my sister. Where is she, by the way? Is she still here?"

Hassan ignored the question. "Are you a thief?"

"No, of course not. I told you, I want to buy a present for my mum. I was looking for more carpets."

"You are lying," said Hassan. "What is the truth?"

"I've already told you the truth," said Ben. "I want to go now. I've got to go and find my sister." He tried to make his way towards the door, but Yusuf and Elias wouldn't let him pass. He knew there was no point trying to struggle. He couldn't fight two strong men. He said, "If you don't let me go, I'm going to call the police."

Hassan laughed. "You are a thief. You want the police?"

"Yes, I do."

"No police," said Hassan. "You will talk to me. You say you have six hundred dollars. Where is it? Where is the money?"

Ben tried to protest, demanding that he should be allowed to find his sister and call his father, but Hassan cut him off, snarling an order to his sons. Elias grabbed Ben's right arm and twisted it behind his back.

Ben yelped. "Ow! That hurts! Get off!"

Elias jerked his arm ever higher.

Ben gritted his teeth against the pain. If he struggled, he'd pull his own arm out of its socket.

Yusuf went through Ben's pockets and found nothing but a cheap plastic lighter. He passed it to his father.

Hassan turned the lighter over and over in his hands as if he was searching for some hidden significance. He flicked the flint and let the flame burn for a few seconds. Then he stared at Ben. He sensed there was something wrong, but he didn't know what. "You have no money?"

"My sister," gasped Ben. "She's got it."

"Tell me the truth, please." Hassan stepped closer, the flame still blazing in his hand. "I want to know the truth. Only the truth. Who are you?"

36

Inspector Mahmoud didn't want to be disturbed.

At this time of the afternoon, he always lay down on the floor of his office, placed a handkerchief over his face and had a short snooze. His men knew what he was doing and they were careful to leave him alone.

Today was different.

This afternoon, to the inspector's intense irritation, he had barely settled himself on the floor when one of his junior officers rapped on the door, apologized for the interruption and explained that two foreigners needed to speak to him about a very urgent matter.

Inspector Mahmoud wondered what could possibly be more urgent than his nap, but he followed his colleague back to the main lobby, where he found Robert, Celia, the two plain-clothes policemen and the boy who he had personally locked up earlier that day.

For a moment, Inspector Mahmoud wondered if he was still asleep. Was this a dream? Then he fired a series of questions at Tariq, demanding to know what was going on.

Tariq pursed his lips and refused to talk.

"He's been like this the whole time," explained Robert. "He won't tell us anything."

"No problem," said Inspector Mahmoud. "Come with me."

He led them through the corridors and down a flight of stairs to the basement, where he quizzed the officer on duty, asking why he hadn't reported an escaped prisoner.

For one simple reason, explained the officer. No prisoners had escaped. In fact, he had just toured the cells, looking through the peepholes at the prisoners, and every one of them was present and correct. Including the boy called Tariq.

"How can he be there?" cried Inspector Mahmoud. "He's here!"

"He's not here," said the officer. "He's there!"

Inspector Mahmoud pulled a handkerchief from his pocket and mopped his forehead. Then he ordered the officer to lead him straight to Tariq's cell.

37

Ben wished he knew karate.

He'd hurl Hassan over the desk, spin round and kick Elias in the head, then land a two-handed punch in the middle of Yusuf's belly.

Splat! Crack! Thump!

And he'd be free.

But Ben could only fight like that on a computer.

In real life, he'd never done more than kick his little sister in the shins or punch a boy at school who flicked him with a wet towel. Not exactly good preparation for disabling three strong men.

He remembered what Tariq had said about Hassan and how brutally he took revenge on anyone foolish enough to try and cheat him. For the first time, Ben felt scared. Up to now, sneaking into the cellar and robbing the safe had seemed like a game. He'd never paused to consider the consequences. Now he looked at the angry faces of the three men surrounding him and wondered how he would get out of here alive.

Kitkat knew he was here. Frank too. Would they come and rescue him?

It didn't seem very likely.

He'd have to save himself. If he couldn't do it by force – and he knew he couldn't – then he'd have to talk his way out of here.

"I'll tell you whatever you want to know," he said. "Can you just ask your son to let me go? He's really hurting my arm."

Hassan considered this request, then shook his head. "First, you talk. Then you go. Who are you?"

"My name is Ben."

"You are American?"

"My father is, but my mother's English."

"Why are you here?"

"Because of Tariq."

"Tariq?"

"The boy who was here before."

Hassan took a moment to digest this unexpected information. "You know this boy?"

"I wouldn't say I know him, but I've met him. He helped me."

"How?"

"I'm staying here with my father," said Ben. He

tried to adjust his position, easing the pain and getting the blood flowing back into his arm, but Elias was holding him so tightly that he couldn't move at all. "Last night, we went to a café. We were sitting in the big square, the Jemma Whatever-it's-called. My father has a nice camera. Brand new. It's quite expensive, actually, and very good. He took some photos and then he put the camera on the table. Next time he looked, it had disappeared. Just vanished. He hadn't seen anyone take it. Nor had we. Someone must have walked past the table and picked it up and stolen it. We didn't see who did it. Anyway, we were searching for it and we got talking to a boy. He said his name was Tariq and he could help us."

"He is a thief," said Hassan.

"He said you were."

"Me?" Hassan laughed. "He said what?"

"He said you steal from tourists. He said you'd have our dad's camera. He said we should come here and look around and we'd find it."

"You think I am a thief?"

"I'm just telling you what Tariq told me."

Hassan laughed. "I sell carpets. I have nice plates and fine bowls and some beautiful antiques, all for a good price. I am a shopkeeper. Nothing more."

"Like I said, it's just what Tariq told me."

"So you come here for what? To steal your camera from me?"

"No."

Hassan pointed at the curtain that led into the kitchen. "You think your camera is there?"

"No."

"So why are you there?"

"I was just looking."

Hassan stared at him.

Examined by those piercing eyes, Ben felt uncomfortable and even guilty. He couldn't help worrying that Hassan could see right through him and discover, deep inside him, the lies that he had been telling and the truth that he had been trying to conceal.

Maybe Hassan really did see something like that, because he was struck by a sudden worry. Telling his sons to keep their grip on Ben, he hurried to his desk, opened the top left-hand drawer and pushed his arm inside. He couldn't find what he was searching for. He pulled out the entire drawer and tipped it upside down on his desk, spilling out a sloppy pyramid of papers and envelopes, rubber bands and pencils, but no keys. His face hardened. He threw the drawer aside and rushed back to Ben.

"Where is it?"

Ben tried to look innocent. "Where's what?"

"The key. My key. Where is it?"

"I don't know what you're talking about."

Hassan raised his right hand. "Where is the key?"

Ben realized he'd have to tell the truth. He nodded at the curtain that led to the kitchen. "They're in there. Look in the teapot and you'll find them."

Yusuf rushed into the kitchen and returned a moment later, jangling the big bunch of keys. He spoke to his father in Arabic. Ben guessed that he was telling Hassan about the carpet on the floor. He wondered how well he had replaced it and whether they could tell that he had opened the trapdoor and gone down to the cellar.

Hassan turned back to Ben. "Why do you take my key?"

"Tariq said you had a safe in the kitchen. He said the camera would be there. But I couldn't find it."

"What have you taken?"

"Nothing."

Hassan raised his hand again, ready to land a brutal blow against Ben's face. "Tell me!"

"I've already told you, I haven't taken anything. I couldn't find your safe."

"The truth! Tell me the truth! Or I will—"

The door opened, spilling a shaft of sunlight into the shop, and Kitkat stepped inside. She called out in a cheery voice, "Oh! You're here! I've been looking for you everywhere." Then she took in the scene: Ben pinned and captive, the three men surrounding him and Hassan's raised hand, ready to strike. Her eyes widened. "What's going on?"

"Leave us," hissed Hassan.

"What are you doing to my brother?"

"Just talking."

"You're not talking, you're torturing him! Let him go!"

Hassan didn't respond immediately. He glanced at his sons and Ben, deciding what to do. Then he nodded to Yusuf and gave a curt instruction in Arabic.

Yusuf hurried towards the door.

Kitkat could see what they were planning to do. Push her out, lock the door. And attack Ben. She couldn't let that happen. She stepped backwards so she was standing on the threshold between the shop and the street. Half-turning her head, she shouted so loudly that the lid rattled on the teapot:

"HELP!"

Elias and Yusuf looked at their father, waiting for his instructions. Should they throw the girl outside and slam the door? Or bring her inside and shut her up?

Hassan didn't know what to do.

He knew how to deal with men. And women too. He either paid them or he punched them.

But he had no idea how to deal with a seven-year-old girl.

Especially one with such strong lungs.

Seeing that they hadn't released Ben and showed no signs of doing so, Kitkat took another deep breath and yelled again:

"HEEEEEEEELP!"

Hassan realized he had no choice. He had to stop her. He called out to Yusuf, who darted towards Kitkat, ready to grab her and put his hand over her mouth.

Kitkat was too quick for him. She dodged out of his reach, stepped out of the door and screamed once more:

"HEEEEEEEEEEEEEEEELP!"

There was an answering commotion outside. Local shopkeepers and passing pedestrians had come to see what was happening. A fist hammered on the door and voices shouted for Hassan, ordering him to come outside and explain himself.

It was lucky that the street was hidden from Hassan and his sons, because they would have seen that the crowd was being urged into action by a scrawny boy wearing black jeans, black socks, black plimsolls, a black T-shirt and a pair of black-rimmed glasses.

Frank was calling on everyone within earshot to help that poor, powerless little girl.

If Yusuf could have seen him, he might have remembered a boy who had been lurking in the shadows just before he went flying. And then he might have wondered why so many foreign children were hanging around the shop. Why one of them had tripped him up and another was shouting for the police and a third appeared to have stolen the keys to the cellar.

A woman yelled. The crowd surged forward. Everyone wanted to know why that foreign girl wouldn't stop screaming.

Hassan realized he had no choice. The police would arrive in a few moments, drawn by the crowd, and he didn't want them in his shop. They'd ask too many questions. He nodded to Elias, who released Ben.

"Go! Go!" Hassan waved Ben towards the doorway. "And never come back!"

"Don't worry," said Ben. "I won't."

He ran out of the door.

Up ahead, he could see Kitkat. And there was Frank, standing at the edge of the crowd, waiting for them.

Hands reached for Ben and voices called out to him, asking questions that he couldn't understand. He could feel fingers pawing his clothes. He ducked under outstretched arms and pushed through the crowd.

When the three of them were together, they didn't bother talking. Getting away was more important. They sprinted past the spice stall and continued down the alleyway, wanting to put as much distance as possible between themselves and Hassan.

In normal circumstances, Ben could have outpaced the others, but he was limping.

Kitkat asked, "What have they done to your leg?"

"Don't worry," said Ben. "I've just got something in my shoe."

"Let's stop and you can take it out."

They were far enough from the shop now. It was safe. Ben stopped, knelt down and undid his laces. He pulled off his shoe and tipped it up, holding out his hand to catch the object that fell out.

"Is it a stone?" asked Kitkat.

"It's three stones."

Ben opened his palm to reveal the ring.

38

Ben, Frank and Kitkat hurried through the alleyways, glancing over their shoulders to check that they weren't being followed. They soon arrived in the Jemma al Fna. They stayed hidden in the shadows for a moment, searching for any sign of Hassan or his sons, then dodged through the crowds and sprinted across the square to the police station.

They crashed through the swinging wooden doors and entered the lobby. A tourist was sitting on the wooden bench with his head in his hands. A lawyer was arguing with his client and two thieves were protesting their innocence to the plain-clothes policemen who had arrested them.

Ben marched straight past all of them and placed his hands on the counter. "Excuse me? *Excusez-moi?* We want to see Inspector Mahmoud."

A uniformed policeman was sitting behind the

desk. He glanced at Ben, then shook his head. "That is not possible."

"Why not?"

"Inspector Mahmoud is not available. You must talk to me. What is your business?"

"He's holding a prisoner," said Ben. "We want her to be released."

"Him," hissed Kitkat.

"Oh, yes." Ben corrected himself. "We want *him* to be released."

The policeman was puzzled. "Him? Her? Who is who?"

"Just fetch Inspector Mahmoud," said Ben. "Tell him we've found the diamond thief. He'll know what you're talking about."

The policeman thought for a moment. He knew about the urchin who had been arrested twice in one day and the Americans who had lost their diamond ring. If these children really did know what had happened, Inspector Mahmoud would want to see them immediately. He lifted the receiver of an old black telephone and dialled a number.

Ten minutes later, the entire police station was in a state of uproar.

A large crowd had gathered in the lobby. There

were uniformed police and plain-clothes police and traffic wardens and secretaries and lawyers. They had been joined by a disorderly drunk, a couple of pickpockets in handcuffs and a tourist who had lost his wallet.

Robert was there, of course, with Celia beside him. Tariq was pinned between two burly policemen, who were determined that he shouldn't get any clever ideas about trying to escape. Harmony had been fetched from her cell. They had come to the main desk to meet Ben, Frank and Kitkat. Now all of them were talking at once.

Inspector Mahmoud fished in his pockets for a handkerchief and wiped the sweat from his forehead.

He had rushed from his office to the lobby and then to the cells, and now he was back in the lobby again, wondering whether to believe what he was hearing. Half of him hoped that he might still be asleep, dreaming the whole thing, but the other half knew that this was worse than any nightmare. He clapped his hands and called for silence, but no one took any notice. Then he took a deep breath and yelled once more, "SILENCE!"

The room went quiet. Only one of the thieves carried on talking, complaining that the whole thing had been a terrible misunderstanding and he'd intended to put his hand into his own pocket, not someone else's. A policeman slapped the back of his head and he shut up too.

"*Merci beaucoup*," said Inspector Mahmoud. "Thank you very much. Now, please, one person will talk. One person and only one person. Him and only him will tell me what is the whole picture. So, who will talk?"

Ben knew as much as anyone, so he stepped forward.

"It's very simple," he said. "We found this."

He pulled the three diamonds from his pocket and held them aloft so they could be seen by everyone.

Then three things happened at once.

Robert cried out, "Is that real?"

Celia clapped her hands with joy. "Oh! Where was it?"

And Ben was knocked off his feet.

The whole crowd pushed forward, ramming into him from every direction. Traffic wardens and pickpockets and tourists and lawyers – all of them wanted to see the ring for themselves.

Ben probably would have been trampled underfoot if Harmony, Frank and Kitkat hadn't surrounded him, making a human barrier to protect him from the forest of hands and arms and fingers, reaching out to touch the ring.

Inspector Mahmoud realized that they couldn't continue this conversation in public. Not without a riot. They went to his office, where Robert took the ring from Ben and placed it safely in a pocket of his own jeans.

The inspector sat behind his desk, ordered one of his junior officers to bring tea and pastries for everyone, and asked Ben to explain the day's events.

Ben told him what he knew. The others interrupted occasionally, adding details which Ben hadn't witnessed himself.

When Ben finished, Inspector Mahmoud sat quietly for a moment, his forehead furrowed and his hands clasped around his belly, thinking through what he had just heard. Then he summoned two of his officers, who were waiting in the corridor. He ordered one of them to take six men and search Hassan's shop for stolen goods. He told the other to arrest Tariq.

They didn't immediately understand what was happening, because the inspector spoke to his men in Arabic. But when one of the policemen unclipped a pair of handcuffs from his belt and made a lunge for Tariq's wrists, Ben demanded to know what was going on. Tariq told him. And Ben protested to the inspector. "Why are you arresting him? What's he done?"

The inspector smiled. "He stole the ring, yes? He is a thief."

"That's not fair," said Harmony.

"He helped us!" cried Kitkat.

"Without him," explained Frank, "we'd never have found the ring."

"Wait a minute," said Celia. "Without him, I never would have lost it."

"That's true," said Ben. "But he helped us get it back again. Doesn't that mean anything?"

Celia thought for a moment. She stared at Tariq as if she was searching for signs of honesty in his eyes.

He stared straight back.

Celia must have found whatever she was looking for, because she nodded. "You're right. He might have been a bad kid, but he's made the effort to redeem himself. He deserves a second chance."

Inspector Mahmoud refused to listen to any arguments. He was determined to put Tariq behind bars for a long, long time. By escaping from prison, the boy had made him look like an idiot.

Following the inspector's orders, the policeman turned Tariq to face the wall, tugged his arms behind his back and snapped the handcuffs on his wrists.

Ben complained and Harmony protested and Frank argued and Kitkat begged, but the inspector refused to be swayed. He had made up his mind and he wasn't going to change it. He ordered the policeman to take Tariq down to the cells.

"Wait a second," said Robert. He stepped between the policeman and the door. "I have a friend called Sadie. She's a writer and she works for the *New York Times*." He looked at Inspector Mahmoud. "Do you know that paper?"

"Of course," said the inspector. "It is very famous."

"She's always looking for stories," said Robert. "I'm going to suggest that she writes about you. Would you mind that?"

"About me?" A broad smile spread across the inspector's face. "Of course, I will be very happy."

"That's great," said Robert. "This is just her kind of story. She's going to love it. The Moroccan boy who escaped from prison. The American girl who took his place. The kids who found a diamond ring. And the police who arrested the wrong guy. Not once, but twice."

Inspector Mahmoud was frowning. "This is not so good, I think."

Now it was Robert's turn to smile. "It's not just good. It's brilliant! You know what? I'm going to ring her right away." He pulled his phone from his pocket.

"Please, you must stop. Your friend, she must not write this story."

"Why not?" asked Robert. "Don't you want to be famous?"

Inspector Mahmoud understood what was being asked of him. Speaking Arabic in a low voice, he ordered the policeman to release Tariq.

The inspector was a sensitive man and he had no desire to be publicly humiliated in one of the world's most prominent newspapers. All charges would be dropped, he promised. Tariq was free to go.

39

Robert wanted to celebrate.

"Celebrate what?" asked Kitkat.

"We've got the ring back. The family's together again. And you've made a new friend. What's not to celebrate? You're the guide, Tariq. Where's the best place to get a drink round here?"

Tariq didn't have to think about it. "The Café de France." He pointed to the other side of the Jemma al Fna, where a three-storey building offered terraces and tables overlooking the square. You could sit there all day, nursing a Coke or a mint tea, and you'd have a perfect view of all the action.

"Perfect," said Robert. "Come on, everyone. Follow me!"

He led them through the Jemma al Fna, ignoring the outstretched hands of one-eyed beggars, the pirouettes of acrobats and the invitations of fortune tellers, promising to predict his future. All he wanted was a drink.

The others hurried after him.

Ben kept his eyes on the crowd, searching for any sign of Hassan, Yusuf or Elias. He hadn't forgotten them and he was sure that they hadn't forgotten him either. What if the police didn't catch them in time? What if they couldn't find enough evidence to tie Hassan to any crimes? What if he and his sons decided to grab some old swords or a curved dagger and take revenge on the foreigners who had humiliated them?

If that happened, Ben would be ready for them.

While they were walking, Harmony took Celia aside and apologized to her.

She didn't have to explain what she was apologizing for. Celia knew already. Robert had told her everything.

"It was stupid of me," said Harmony. "I wasn't thinking. Of course you wouldn't steal your own ring. I'm really sorry."

"You don't have to worry," said Celia in a soft voice, putting her hand on Harmony's arm. "Listen, honey, I know what this is all about."

"Do you?"

"Of course I do. I wouldn't expect you to want me to marry your dad. But can I ask you a favour? Give me some time. Don't judge me before you know me. You never know, you might even like having me as your stepmother. Do you think there's any chance of that?"

Harmony didn't answer immediately. She bit her lip, wondering whether to say what she really felt. Telling the truth had already caused enough trouble for one day. Eventually, she said, "Can I ask you a personal question?"

"You can ask me anything. But I don't promise to answer it."

"How old are you?"

"Twenty-six," said Celia.

"Do you know how old my dad is?"

"Of course I do."

"He's almost twice your age."

"That's a slight exaggeration."

"Don't you think you're a bit young for him?"

"No, I don't," said Celia. "I think we're absolutely suited to one another. He's got a young mind in a old body and I've got an old mind in a young body."

Harmony winced. "I don't want to hear about Dad's body. Or yours."

"I'm sorry, honey. When you're a bit older, you'll understand."

"I understand everything already," said Harmony. "You're after his money, aren't you?"

For a second, Celia was so surprised that she couldn't speak. Then she threw back her head and cackled with laughter.

"What's so funny?" said Harmony.

"You really think I'm marrying your dad for his money?"

"I know you are," said Harmony.

"Do you know how much he earns?"

"No."

"I do. And I can tell you, his annual income isn't even one tenth of mine."

"He bought you a very expensive ring."

Celia sighed. "Harmony, I don't want to be the one who blows the cobwebs away from your pretty little eyes, but you're not giving me much choice. I paid for that ring."

Harmony wasn't sure that she'd heard correctly. "You paid for your own engagement ring?"

"Your dad is having some cash-flow problems. I paid for our flights. I paid for the riad too. If you want to know the truth, this whole holiday is on me. I'm a very successful actress, Harmony, and I earn an excellent wage. Don't look so shocked. This is the twenty-first century. I don't need to be looked after by a man. I can look after myself – and him too."

Now Harmony was completely bewildered. "I don't understand. If you're not after Dad's money, why do you want to marry him?"

"It's very simple," said Celia. "Because I love him."

40

The Café de France has three floors. The ground floor is used mostly by locals drinking coffee, doing deals and exchanging gossip. The middle floor offers shade and a fine view of the Jemma al Fna. On the top floor, the view is even better, but you're exposed to the sun's fierce glare.

The Misfitz didn't mind. They loved the sun. Anyway, they were already shielded by hats, glasses and generous dollops of sunscreen, smeared over their faces, necks and arms.

Robert chose a table by the edge of the terrace. From the comfort of their chairs, they could see all the action in the Jemma al Fna. Down there, two hustlers were trying to persuade a tourist to have his picture taken with a monkey balanced on his forearm. Over there, a dentist was displaying a big box of pulled teeth and a rusty pair of pliers, offering to cure anyone's toothache. Directly under their terrace, a little old woman strapped bulging bags of shopping on to the back of a donkey.

Robert leaned back in his chair, positioning himself so the sunshine played over his face, and rubbed his hands together. "Oh, this is perfect. All is well with the world and we're on holiday! Finally we can have some fun. How about a drink? A serious drink. I'm tired of tea. Shall we crack open a bottle of champagne?"

Harmony shook her head in dismay. "Dad, you're an alcoholic."

"No, I'm not. I just know how to enjoy myself. Why don't you join me? You're old enough, aren't you?"

"No, thanks."

"Go on. Just a little glass. It won't kill you."

"I said no. Anyway, we're in a Muslim country. They won't sell champagne here."

"It's worth a try," said Robert. He summoned the waiter and asked for a bottle of their finest bubbly. To his irritation, he discovered that Harmony was right. The Café de France did not serve alcohol. Robert sighed and ordered mint tea and some food for everyone. No one had eaten lunch.

Harmony and Tariq went to the loos and

swapped clothes. By the time they came back, the waiter had already delivered six small glasses and a silver teapot stuffed with fresh mint leaves. He returned with a big basket of bread and a long tray stacked with snacks: black olives, green chillies, sliced tomatoes, cubed cucumber, mushy aubergine, pickled turnip, tiny skewers of grilled lamb and little squares of hot pizza, dribbling melted cheese.

As they made their way through the pizza and the kebabs, they discussed the day's events, filling in the missing pieces for one another, and then they quizzed Tariq, asking what he was planning to do next. After today's escapades, surely he couldn't carry on working for Hassan. If he was sensible, he wouldn't even stay in Marrakech. So where would he go?

"Home," said Tariq. "To my mother and my father."

"How will you get there?" asked Ben.

"I will walk."

"I thought you said it was a hundred kilometres."

Tariq shrugged his shoulders. "No problem. I have strong feet."

"What about the donkey?" asked Kitkat. "I

thought you were going to stay in Marrakech till you earned enough to buy a donkey."

"This city is not safe for me," said Tariq. "I must go home."

They quizzed Tariq about his village and his family. He pointed in the general direction of the mountains and explained that he lived in a small house in a quiet valley, a morning's walk from the nearest town. He shared a bedroom with his two brothers and four sisters. Their house had neither electricity nor running water. Every morning, before breakfast, they carried buckets to a well and fetched enough water to last the whole day.

"Not like here," said Tariq, gesturing at the city that surrounded them. "It is very *pauvre*. Understand?"

"Poor," said Harmony.

"Yes. Very poor."

Celia whispered in Robert's ear. Following her suggestion, he opened his wallet and selected several notes. He offered them to Tariq. "Would that pay for a new donkey?"

Tariq stared wide-eyed at the money. "For me?"

"It's a gift," said Robert. "From our family to yours."

Tariq couldn't believe it. He gingerly took the

money from Robert's outstretched hand, then glanced at the other customers in the café, checking if any of them had noticed. He didn't trust anyone. Then he stuffed the notes quickly into his shorts and thanked Robert.

"Forget it," said Robert. "Just say hi to your dad from me. I hope he likes his new donkey."

Tariq stood up. It was time to leave. If Hassan, Yusuf and Elias hadn't been caught by the police, they would be looking for him already.

Harmony asked for his address. She wanted to send him a postcard from London. Tariq couldn't write English or French, only Arabic, but he scrawled a few words on a paper napkin.

"I'll get someone to translate it," said Harmony. "Then I'll write to you. We all will."

Tariq smiled. "Very good. Thank you."

"Will you write back?" asked Kitkat.

"*Bien sûr*. Of course."

Tariq went round the table, saying goodbye to everyone and thanking them for their help.

Finally he returned to Robert and shook his hand once more, then wrapped him in a warm embrace. "Thank you, Monsieur Robert. Thank you. A thousand times, thank you."

Robert chuckled, not sure whether to be pleased

or embarrassed. "Don't mention it. I'm just happy to help."

"You are a good man," said Tariq. Releasing Robert, he took a step backwards and looked once more around the group as if he was memorizing all their faces. Then he turned and hurried towards the stairs that led out of the café.

They watched him, waiting for him to look back and wave, but he never did. He just trotted down the stairs and disappeared.

When he had gone, Kitkat said, "Do you think we'll ever see him again?"

"I hope so," said Celia. "He was a sweet kid."

"I'm going to write to him," said Harmony.

"He'll never write back," said Ben.

"He can't even write English," added Kitkat.

"Even if he could," said Frank, "he probably lives ten miles from the nearest postbox."

"I don't care what you all think." Harmony folded the paper napkin and tucked it carefully into her pocket. "I'm going to write to him anyway."

"Honey?" Celia leaned across the table and laid her hand on Robert's arm. "Could I have my ring back now?"

Robert smiled. "Of course, darling."

He pushed his hand into his pocket. His face

fell. He checked his other pocket. Now he was looking worried. He jumped to his feet and patted all four pockets of his jeans, front and back, then dug his fingers into his shirt pocket too, but he couldn't find what he was looking for.

Harmony said, "Dad? What's going on?"

"Nothing. Don't worry. It's all fine."

"You haven't. . ." Celia could barely bring herself to say the words. "You haven't lost my ring, have you?"

"I can't find it, that's all. Give me a minute." Robert tried all his pockets again, then ran his fingers through his curly hair. "This is insane. I can't have lost it."

Harmony said, "When did you last see it?"

"When Ben gave it to me."

"You're sure you haven't seen it since then?"

"I haven't *seen* it. But I *felt* it in my pocket."

"When did you last feel it?"

"Just now. In the square. Before we came up here."

"It must have fallen out of your pocket. We've got to search the café." Harmony pushed back her chair. "Let's divide up. We should start right now before someone else has a chance to find it."

The others were just about to join her when Ben

stopped them. "There's no point searching anything. I know where the ring is."

They all turned to look at him.

"Tariq took it," said Ben.

41

There was a moment of shocked silence, followed by a hubbub of questions. Everyone shouted at once, but Robert was the loudest. "Give him a chance! Let him speak!" When the others had quietened down, Robert nodded to his son. "Go on, Ben. You sound very confident. How can you be so sure he took it?"

"I don't *know* he took it. But I bet he did. He's been cheating us from the very beginning."

"Why would he take the ring? I've just given him some money."

"He's greedy," explained Ben. "That's why he stole the ring in the first place. Hassan took it from him. He used us to get it back again. And now he's stolen it again."

"I don't understand," said Kitkat. "Is he a goodie or a baddie?"

"Maybe he's a bit of both," replied Frank.

Robert still wasn't convinced. "There's one fatal flaw, Sherlock. Tariq might have been a good thief, but even he couldn't have taken the ring from my pocket. He barely shook my hand."

"That's not true," said Ben. "He hugged you. And he's a brilliant pickpocket." He explained how Tariq had taken his phone. Frank and Kitkat confirmed what he was saying.

Harmony had a sudden thought. "I wonder if Tariq has been telling the truth about anything." She hurried across the terrace to the waiter and showed him the napkin, asking him to translate the words for her.

She came back and delivered the bad news. "This isn't his address. It's just a bunch of squiggles which don't mean anything."

"This is terrible!" cried Kitkat. "How are we going to find him?"

"You're not," replied Robert.

"We've got to try!"

"No, you haven't."

"What do you mean? We can't just let him get away with it!"

"Keep cool, Kitkat. Stop shouting at me, I'm right here. Can you sit down, please? And the rest of you. Back in your seats. Thank you. Now, I'm going to go to the police station and talk to Inspector Mahmoud. Tariq can't have run far. He's only a few minutes ahead of us. I know you'd prefer to catch him yourselves, but we're going to enlist the assistance of the police."

"The police are useless!" cried Kitkat.

"She's right," said Ben. "They'll never find him."

"This is their country," said Robert. "I know you have a low opinion of their expertise, but they know what they're doing. Celia, can you look after the kids? Don't let them go anywhere. They've had enough adventures for one day. I'll be back in a few minutes and I want to find all of you right here at this table."

42

When Robert had gone, the Misfitz sat in angry silence, staring at the Jemma al Fna. Celia made a few attempts to chat, but no one responded with more than a grunt. They weren't interested in making polite conversation. They wanted to be out there in the city, hunting through the streets, scouring the souk, asking questions and uncovering evidence, searching for Tariq and the ring.

All four of them were furious. They felt bitter and betrayed. They hadn't just devoted time and energy to helping Tariq; they had treated him like a friend. One of the family. An honorary member of the Misfitz. Harmony had even spent half a day in prison so he could be free.

And how had he repaid them?

With thievery and cheating.

He had made them look like idiots.

He'd made them feel like idiots too.

In fact, thought Ben, we *are* idiots. It was our fault for trusting him. We should have known he'd try to con us again.

Once a thief, always a thief.

Ben leaned on the balcony with his chin in his hands.

Directly below him, he could see Robert emerging from the ground floor of the café and hurrying across the square, swerving to avoid touts and beggars. He watched his father till he was lost amongst the crowd.

He stared at the seething mass of humanity – the tourists and the locals, the dancers and the musicians, the taxi drivers and the donkey riders – hoping he might catch a sudden glimpse of a skinny boy with black hair, grubby trousers and a grey hoodie. But he knew it was hopeless. Tariq wouldn't stick around the Jemma al Fna. Too many people were looking for him. He wouldn't even stay in the city. That was why the police didn't have a hope of finding him. By now, he would be walking along the road that led to the mountains and his father's village, his thumb stuck out, trying to hitch a lift from passing cars.

Or would he?

Ben remembered what Tariq had said earlier in the day.

He had talked about his hopes for the future, his dreams of wealth and exploration. He had imagined a glorious future for himself, venturing to France or Spain, living in Paris or Madrid, working hard and making his fortune. He hadn't even mentioned going home to his village.

Ben told the others what he had remembered. "He doesn't want to go home to his father and his family. He wants to get out of Marrakech and go to Europe."

Harmony said, "Maybe, just maybe, he wasn't telling the truth."

"I think he was. That's why he took the ring. With the money that Dad gave him, he'd be able to go back to his own village and buy a new donkey. But with the ring, he could go to Europe and start a new life for himself."

"Ring your dad," said Kitkat. "Tell the police to check the airport."

"He couldn't go by plane," said Frank. "I'm sure he doesn't have a passport. Even if he does, he won't have a visa."

"So how's he going to get to Europe?"

"Don't ask me," said Frank.

Ben had already thought it through. "Remember what he said before? He was planning to go to Casablanca. A big city is a good place to hide. When he's there, he could sell the diamonds and get a passport. Then he can go to Madrid, Paris, London, New York – wherever he wants."

"You have to tell your dad," said Kitkat. "The police shouldn't be looking for Tariq here. They'll have to find him in Casablanca."

"He won't have got there yet," said Frank. "It's more than a hundred miles away."

"We could go to the bus station and stop him," suggested Ben. He glanced at Celia. "If we weren't stuck here."

"You are stuck here," said Celia. "Your father was very clear about that."

Ben said, "Wouldn't he be pleased if we found the ring?"

"I'm sure he'd be delighted, but that's not the point."

"What is the point?"

"The point is," said Celia and then paused as if she wasn't quite sure what she had intended to say. She bit her lip and looked around the table at the four children. Then she shook her head. "I can't," she said. "I'm very sorry, but I just can't. He'd be furious."

"Not if we find the ring," said Ben.

"What if you don't?"

"We will."

"Your father was very clear. He said I had to keep you here."

"We'll be fine," promised Harmony. "We know what we're doing. We're perfectly capable of looking after ourselves."

Celia was wavering. "Maybe we should call him and ask what he thinks. If you ask his permission, maybe he'll let you go to the bus station."

"He won't," said Ben. "You know he won't. He thinks the police will find Tariq. But he's wrong. They haven't got a clue what they're doing. If we leave it to the police, I promise you, your ring will be broken up and the silver will be melted down and the three diamonds will be sold in three different jewellery shops in Casablanca."

Celia thought for a moment. Then she laughed and shook her head. "I'm going to regret this." She opened her purse, pulled out all her money and handed it to Ben. "That should be enough for a taxi to the station. And back again. Because you're going to come straight back here, aren't you?"

"Of course we will," said Ben, taking the money.

Kitkat clapped her hands and Harmony said, "Thank you, Celia. Thank you so much."

"Forget it." Celia shooed them away. "Just go! Before I change my mind."

They sprinted down the three flights to the ground floor of the Café de France, then raced across the square to the taxis.

Ben jumped into the car at the front of the queue. The others scrambled onto the back seat after him. The driver turned to look at them, waiting to hear their destination.

"We want to go the bus station," said Ben.

"One hundred dirhams," said the driver.

Frank chuckled. "That's insane. We'll give you twenty."

"No, no. You must pay one hundred."

"Twenty-five," offered Frank.

"Eighty."

"Thirty."

"Sixty."

Ben extracted two notes from the bundle that he had been given by Celia and waved them under the driver's nose. "If you get us there in ten minutes, you can have two hundred dirhams."

"Ten minutes? To the bus station? This is impossible!"

"Don't you want two hundred dirhams?"

The driver glanced at the notes to check that they were genuine, then decided not to argue. He released the handbrake and jammed his foot on the accelerator. The little yellow taxi sprang forward, pressing everyone against their seats, and skidded through the traffic, leaving a trail of braking cars and swerving bicycles and shocked donkeys and outraged pedestrians, who cursed and yelled and waved their fists.

Clinging to her seat, Kitkat shouted across the taxi to her sister, "I know you don't want her to marry your dad. But if you've got to have a stepmother, she seems like a pretty good one."

"She's not bad," said Harmony.

The others stared at her in amazement, wondering why she had changed her mind. Harmony didn't explain. She just leaned forward and tapped the driver on his shoulder. "*Vite! Vite! Vous comprenez?*"

"*Oui, mademoiselle, je conduis le plus vite possible!*"

43

They reached the bus station in nine minutes and forty-three seconds. Ben thrust the two notes in the driver's hands and leaped out of the taxi, followed by the others. The driver shouted his thanks after them, but the Misfitz took no notice. They had more important things to think about.

The bus station was a modern complex with a large ticket office and about twenty or thirty buses collecting or unloading passengers. Neat shelters protected travellers from the sun. Men wandered along the queues, selling drinks, fruit, cigarettes and chewing gum. Thirty or forty taxis waited in a line. A couple of camels were roped to a lamp post. Stray dogs wandered through the crowds, searching for scraps.

There must have been timetables and an information desk in the ticket office, but Ben didn't have time to find them. He just ran to the nearest bus and called up to the driver. "Excuse me? Are you going to Casablanca?"

"Casa?" The driver shook his head, jerked his thumb down the line and muttered in French.

Ben couldn't understand him, but Harmony did. "He said it's this way. And it's just about to leave."

They sprinted down the line of buses, quizzing the drivers, shouting questions in French and English, till someone pointed out the bus for Casablanca.

The door was shut, the exhaust was gushing fumes and the bus was nudging through the crowd, heading for the main road.

Harmony sighed.

Kitkat despaired.

Frank lifted his phone and took a picture of the bus's number plate.

And Ben ran.

He didn't tell the others what he was doing. He didn't think about them at all. In fact, he didn't think about anything except running. His lungs pumped oxygen, his arms whirled through the air and his feet pounded on the tarmac. He dodged around a cart stacked with oranges, pushed past a group of women in white robes, vaulted over a big leather suitcase and hurled himself in front of the bus, throwing his hands in the air and shouting, "Stop!"

The bus ploughed onwards, bearing down on him, the big wheels grinding in the dust. For a moment, he thought he'd made a terrible mistake. What sort of idiot throws himself in front of a bus?

Then the driver slammed his foot on the brake and the bus shuddered to a standstill, stopping so close to Ben's face that he saw his own startled eyes reflected in the windscreen, staring back at him.

Inside the bus, passengers protested and the driver shouted down at Ben, telling him to get out of the way.

Ben walked round to the door and rapped on the glass.

The driver pressed a button and the door slid open.

Ben shouted up to him, "Are you going to Casablanca?"

He was.

Ben clambered up the steps and peered down the length of the bus. Passengers stared back at him. He could see old men with beards and women in headscarves and a young man in military uniform and a woman with a baby and, right at the back of the bus, a skinny boy with black hair – and then he was gone, ducking behind the seats.

Too late, thought Ben. I've seen you.

He hurried down the aisle.

He hadn't taken more than a single step when an arm shot out and held him back. The bus driver yelled at him in a language that he couldn't understand.

"I'm sorry," said Ben. "I don't know what you're saying."

The driver waved his right hand. "*Billet! Billet!*"

"You need a ticket," explained Harmony. She and the others had raced after Ben and were now standing at the bottom of the steps.

"Tell him I'm not going anywhere," said Ben. "I just want to talk to someone. Do I really need a ticket for that?"

Harmony stepped aboard and spoke to the driver in French. Then she translated for Ben. "He says the bus is leaving right now. If you're not travelling, you have to get off."

"Can't he wait for a second?"

"No."

"Tell him there's a thief on board."

"I have. He doesn't care."

"Fine." Ben pulled out his money. "I'll buy a ticket. How much is it?"

"What about us?" protested Kitkat.

Ben sighed and gave the money to Harmony. "You'd better buy four."

Frank and Kitkat stepped aboard. Harmony handed over the cash and the driver presented her with four grubby pink paper stubs.

The door eased shut with a hiss and a click. The bus lurched forward. They were on their way to Casablanca.

44

Tariq knew he couldn't hide or escape, so he shuffled along his seat, making room, and greeted them like long-lost friends. "Hello! Welcome! You are coming to Casa?"

No one replied immediately. Ben sat beside Tariq. Frank, Harmony and Kitkat took the surrounding seats. Other passengers eyed them curiously, wondering why four foreigners had joined the bus so suddenly and come to sit beside a local boy.

Ben decided that there was no point making polite chit-chat or trying to be clever. Better to get straight down to business. "Where's the ring?"

Tariq peered at him, puzzled. "Excuse me? I do not understand."

"The diamonds," said Ben. "Where are the diamonds?"

"I have no diamonds."

"We know you took them again."

"Me?"

"Yes, you."

Tariq's face was a picture of shocked innocence. "No, no, no. I help you find them. Why do I take them?"

"That's a good question," said Ben. "I'd be really interested to know the answer. Why did you take them? And where are they now?"

"I tell you, I don't take them. It is not me. This is one big mistake."

Frank stepped in with a question. "You told us you were planning to go back to your village. So what are you doing on this bus?"

"My plans, they change," said Tariq. "I speak to my father. He is now in Casa. I must to visit him there."

"Why is he in Casablanca?" asked Harmony.

"To see the doctor."

"Which doctor?"

"One very good doctor. The best in Casa."

Frank said, "You told us he didn't have enough money to pay for doctors."

"My cousin, he gives him the money." Tariq beamed a big, confident smile. "It is good, no? My father, he will soon be well."

Tariq had an answer for everything, but Ben suspected that all of them were lies. He said, "If you're telling the truth, you won't mind if we search your stuff?"

"Please, search. No problem."

Tariq turned out his pockets. He had a packet of chewing gum, some coins and the money that he had been given by Robert.

Ben tipped Tariq's battered old rucksack on to the seat between them and went through his belongings piece by piece, carefully inspecting each of them. Tariq didn't own anything of value, just a few clothes, a spare pair of sandals and a little plastic torch. He had also packed some food for the journey: two little round loaves, some greasy black olives wrapped in newspaper and a tin of sardines.

Ben opened the torch and tipped out the batteries. He looked at the food, wondering what to do, then realized that he didn't have any choice. If he was going to search everything properly, he'd have to destroy Tariq's lunch. He squeezed each olive and ripped both loaves apart, making sure that nothing had been hidden under the crust, but there was no sign of the ring.

The others watched in nervous silence. When Ben tore up the last piece of bread, Kitkat sighed deeply and put her head in her hands. "Oh, no. I don't believe it! What are we going to do?"

"We should get off the bus and go back to the Café de France," said Frank. "The ring was probably on the floor all the time."

Harmony said, "I'll ask the driver to stop."

She got to her feet . . .

. . . but Ben called her back. "Wait!"

He was sure that Frank was wrong. The ring wasn't on the floor of the Café de France. Tariq had stolen it. And he must have hidden it too.

There was only one place left to look.

It would be undignified, unpleasant and uncomfortable, but Ben knew that he had to do it.

He turned to Tariq. "This probably sounds really strange, but would you mind opening your mouth?"

Tariq stared at him. "Excuse me?"

"I'm really sorry about this. I know you've had a bad day and it's mostly been my fault. But could you open your mouth?"

Kitkat said, "Benjy, what are you doing?"

"I want to look inside his mouth."

"Leave him alone," said Harmony. "We've made him suffer enough."

Ben insisted. "I'm not going to hurt you, I

promise. I just want to have a quick look inside. Do you mind?"

Tariq reluctantly opened his mouth, revealing his pink tongue and rows of immaculate white teeth with no fillings.

Ben said, "Could you lift up your tongue, please?"

Tariq's tongue stayed flat.

Ben said, "This is the last thing, I swear. Please, just lift up your tongue."

"That's enough," said Harmony. "Tariq, don't listen to him. You don't have to do anything that you don't want to."

Ben had no choice. He grabbed Tariq's jaw with his right hand and pushed his left hand into Tariq's mouth.

Kitkat cried, "Benjy! You can't do that!"

"Leave him alone!" snapped Harmony.

Ben took no notice of his sisters. He thrust his left hand deeper into the damp darkness under Tariq's tongue.

He could feel a small object touching the tips of his fingers. Curved and smooth and hard as a tooth. He pulled it out.

Wet with saliva, the three diamonds glistened in the sunlight.

45

Tariq was shameless. He didn't even pretend to be embarrassed. He confessed that he had popped the ring in his mouth as soon as he saw Ben climbing onto the bus. Then he grinned cheekily and shrugged his shoulders. "My friends, I must tell you one thing. I take this ring because I have to. You understand?"

"What do you mean?" asked Kitkat. "Why did you have to?"

"Because I am *pauvre*. You are rich. You have everything. I have nothing. I must take this thing for to make my life good."

"You're not poor," said Ben. "Our father gave you some money."

Tariq nodded. "A little money, yes. But I need much money."

"You were meant to use that money to buy a donkey for your father."

Tariq shrugged his shoulders. "Would you like to have one life with *une âne*? Or will you better be rich?"

"Poverty is no excuse for stealing," said Harmony.

"He has nothing," argued Frank. "That ring might be worth fifty thousand dollars. Can't you understand why he wanted to steal it?"

"I can understand why he did it. But that doesn't change the basic fact that stealing is wrong."

"Stealing isn't always wrong."

"Yes, it is."

"If you were dying of thirst, wouldn't you steal a glass of water?"

"Tariq isn't dying. He's just greedy."

"This is all very interesting," interrupted Ben. He could see that his sister and his stepbrother might continue their philosophical discussion for the next four hours, by which time they would have arrived in Casablanca. He wouldn't mind going there one day, but right now, he'd much rather get off the bus at the next stop and return to Marrakech. They were supposed to be driving to the mountains early tomorrow morning and he didn't want to miss that. "We have to make a decision. What are we going to do? We've found the diamonds. Are we going to take Tariq to the police? Or should we just go back to Dad and Celia with the ring and let him go?"

Tariq understood the question and he watched Ben, Harmony, Frank and Kitkat, waiting for their answers. He knew that his fate rested in their hands.

Harmony was the first to speak. "Part of me thinks he should go back to prison," she said. "He is a thief, after all. He's stolen the ring from us. Twice. And he must have stolen a lot of other things from a lot of other people. And, whatever Frank says, stealing is always wrong. But I've spent a few hours in prison myself today and, I can tell you, no one should be locked up in there. Unless they've done something really bad. Like murder. Tariq didn't actually hurt anyone. And maybe, just maybe, he'll behave better in the future. I think we should let him go."

"That's one vote for freedom," said Ben. "Kitkat?"

"He can't go to prison," said Kitkat. "He's only a boy. Children should never, ever be put in prison."

"Two votes for freedom," said Ben. "Frank?"

"He's a bright guy," said Frank. "He might have done some bad things, but he's got a great future. Ten years from now, Tariq might be a millionaire.

He could be running a business, employing hundreds of people. We should let him go to Casablanca and make his fortune."

"Three votes for freedom," said Ben. "Plus me makes four."

46

The bus swerved off the main road, bumped along the gravel and shuddered to a standstill at the edge of a small village.

An old woman was waiting at the side of the road. She had a bulky black bag at her feet.

The door slid open. The woman hauled the bag on to her shoulders, clambered up the steps and offered some crumpled notes to the driver.

A small, skinny boy squeezed past the old woman and jumped out of the bus. He was followed by two girls and two more boys.

The Misfitz had asked the driver to drop them at his next stop. From there, they would find a way to get back to Marrakech. Tariq was going to stay on the bus and go to Casablanca.

They looked at their surroundings: the main road lined with tall palm trees, the traffic zipping past and the ten or twelve desolate houses which made up this tiny village.

"Here," said Harmony. "This is for you." She had scribbled their address on a piece of a paper, which she handed to Tariq. "Maybe you'll just use it to come and rob our house. But I hope you won't. If you ever get to London, and you've stopped stealing, come and visit us."

"I will be in London," said Tariq, sounding entirely confident about his own future. "Now I go to Casa. I make good money. After, I will fly to London and I will see you there. Thank you." He carefully folded the address and tucked it into his pocket.

The driver hooted his horn. The old woman had taken her seat and the bus was ready to leave.

Tariq shook hands with each of them in turn.

"Goodbye."

"*Au revoir.*"

"Good luck."

"*Bonne chance.*"

Tariq turned round and put his foot on the step. He was just about to clamber into the bus when Ben shouted, "Wait!"

Tariq froze.

Ben put his hand in his pocket. The ring was still there.

"Sorry," said Ben. "I just had to check."

"No problem." Tariq stepped on to the bus and hurried down the aisle.

The door eased shut.

Through the windows, they could see Tariq returning to his seat. The driver hooted his horn once again; then the bus drove away in a cloud of dust.

Ben pushed his hand into his pocket and touched the ring again. Just to make sure.

He knew he'd keep doing that till he could deliver the three diamonds safely into Celia's hands.

They sat under a tree. Through the leaves, the sun cast dappled shadows in the dust. Swallows swooped overhead. A donkey stood sadly in one of the fields, nuzzling the hard, dry earth. There were no other signs of life.

It was hot. They had no food and nothing to drink. The village had no shop and even its dozen houses looked unoccupied.

Using Frank's phone, Ben rang his father and told him the good news.

Robert was so delighted to hear that they were safe – and the ring was too – that he couldn't bring himself to be angry. He just asked where they were. He wanted to come and collect them in a taxi.

The bus driver had told them the name of the

village. Ben spelt it out. Robert wrote it down and promised to get there as quickly as possible.

Ben switched off the phone and told the others what his dad had said.

"When will he get here?" asked Harmony.

"An hour," said Ben. "Maybe two."

Kitkat sighed. "What are we going to do for two hours?"

"I've got Scrabble," said Ben.

"Brilliant. Let's have a. . ." Then she realized he was joking. "Oh, Benjy. When are you going to grow up?"

"Before you."

"I doubt it. You might be older than me, but you're much less mature."

Harmony shook her head. "Are you two going to carry on bickering like this till Dad arrives?"

"We don't have anything else to do," said Kitkat.

"Don't worry," said Frank. "Something will happen."

"How do you know?"

"It always does."

DON'T MISS
more exciting